CREEPY CRAWLIES

Kanika had her formal education from Shri Ram College of Commerce, and Hindu College, University of Delhi. Following that, she has been part of the corporate industry as a Learning and Development professional.

During the pandemic, she got the opportunity to externalize her passion for writing – starting with non-fiction essays that were published in a few magazines and still garner good responses on LinkedIn. She moved on to collaborate with several anthologies.

She published her first horror novella *Bikram and Vitthal* in September 2020. Her second book *Memoirs*, themed on personal musings, was released in August 2021. She has been featured on All India Radio's author interview program twice.

When not writing, she is busy performing as a Spoken Word Artist on various social mics and platforms.

CREEPY CRAWLIES

KANIKA SHARMA

hachette INDIA

First published in India in 2025 by Hachette India
(Registered name: Hachette Book Publishing India Pvt. Ltd)
An Hachette UK company
www.hachetteindia.com

1

Print ISBN 978-93-5731-987-4
Ebook ISBN 978-93-5731-490-9

Hachette Book Publishing India Pvt. Ltd
4th & 5th Floors, Corporate Centre,
Plot No. 94, Sector 44, Gurugram 122003, India

Typeset in Lora
by Mukul

MIX
Paper | Supporting responsible forestry
FSC® C010615

Printed and bound in India
by Thomson Press India Ltd.

To Shree Radharani, *the divine muse behind the quiet courage to begin.*

To my mother's prayer, *soundless yet steadfast, cradling this journey long before I knew I'd walk it.*

And to my husband, *for being the silence that let my stories speak.*

Prologue

PREPARE YOURSELF FOR A JOURNEY THROUGH THESE SPINE-CHILLING narratives, where the line between rational and irrational is blurred. The book's name serves as a cautionary notice for you that each story will creep you out with fear of unknown, unseen, and unheard things (we call them crawlies) that might crawl out at night from under your bed. Each story serves as an individual fear-inducing spooky tale that comes from a different folklore, thus ensuring that, in the process, we have a whole checklist of horror folklore and creepy crawlies checked.

Fear! In the shadows of our minds, fear lurks – an ancient, primal force that shapes our actions, fuels our anxieties, and haunts our dreams.

The revered Oxford dictionary classifies fear as both a noun and a verb. As a noun, it refers to an unpleasant emotion generated by the threat of danger, pain, or harm. As a verb, it is to be scared of someone or something because they are likely to be dangerous, painful, or harmful.

Our worst fears can manifest in a variety of forms. It could be as simple as an undesirable situation like acne right before prom night for a girl. Or it could be something really evil – maybe your sinister twin? The fear could be you, yourself, or an ominous secret that you have been guarding for so long. However, fear at its very worst becomes terror, and it often stems from a non-living entity or object like that old almira in your basement, the necklace you bought from a thrifty garage sale, or the unknown thing that resides in your attic and makes muffled noises at night.

Here in *Creepy Crawlies*, each tale is a testament to the power of fear, a reminder that sometimes the greatest horrors are the ones we carry within. The following collection of stories delves into the darkest recesses of human emotion, where every creak, whisper, and shadow could herald impending doom.

Mind you! Some of these stories may trigger some of your phobias for life; be prepared to confront your deepest fears, for in these pages, they come to life:

Chalawa: Two siblings have been keeping each other's secret for years.

Dybbuk: A New Year's resolution turns into a nightmare. Be careful of the promises you make!

Jorōgumo: In this spine-tingling story, seemingly innocent creatures turn into terrifying monsters, straight out of legend.

Zombies: The classic horror of the dead rising from their graves.

Ghoul: Not all Hotel California–inspired road trips are so lovely after all. Some destinations are meant to be left unexplored, and some roads lead only to despair.

Shakchunni: Ever heard of the phrase 'Albatross across the neck'? What if a man is living this horrid fate every day? This relentless torment serves as a grim parable of guilt and retribution.

Chupacabra: Black ravens and black cats are classic messengers of evil, but what about black goats? Well! They represent Satan himself.

Kappa: What is worse than a demon itself? A child demon is stubborn, and once you make a promise to him, you have to keep it.

Ifrit: We have siblings again, but this time we learn that too much love and attachment can take you through hell, quite literally!

Chitauli: Are ghosts and demons the only scary entities in this world? I would say technology might soon take over as a new frontier of terror, where humanity's creations turn against them.

CHALAWA

Chalawa is a supernatural entity based in Indian folklore that has a penchant for trickery and creating illusions. But can only such entities create illusions and trickery?

THE CANAL-FACING D'SOUZA BUNGALOW SEAMLESSLY MERGES INTO its surroundings. Its glass façade, perforations, and unending foliage are fading witnesses to the sundry generations that have passed through its doors. But it wasn't always like this. In its glory days, the mansion, teeming with life, used to experience renovations every Christmas.

However, with Ramsay's only son not being around for so long, the former's spirit was also subdued, making him unable to keep the tradition alive. As a result, the house suffered through some rough times. A sense of foreboding overtook the bungalow. Surrounded by unkempt, overgrown trees, the windows of the house felt darker, filled with dirt. They created shadows that played tricks on your eyes even in broad daylight.

This was, however, about to change. After five long years of waiting, the D'Souza Bungalow was going to be lit up on Christmas; its dark windows dusted off, foliage trimmed, and dried leaves blown away. For the first time in years, it looked less like a forbidden, abandoned castle and more like a beautiful, inviting mansion.

'Mom, I have tried to prepare Dada's favourite *vindaloo*,' Christina chirped.

'Thank you, my darling Chrissy, you've always been the sweetest pea! Since when have you become so proficient in cooking, my darl–' Molly's praises were cut short by the screech of tyres on the front porch.

'They are here! They are here!' Molly heard Ramsay shout. Chrissy ran to the porch, overtaking her Mama, who had become slow with age. The faded blue door of the run-down Maruti Omni slid open, splitting the red text 'Vizag Mental Asylum', revealing the other half of Christina's soul, her twin Christian.

Mr and Mrs D'Souza engulfed a rather hassled-looking Christian in a bear hug. He had left this house in the same van at the tender age of ten, and today he returned a fine young man of fifteen. Well, 'fine' from the outside at least – just like the newly painted D'Souza Bungalow, the insides of which still bore dents of sordid tales.

Everyone walked Christian inside. Everyone but Christina, who stood there, as if frozen in time, watching her brother with as much joy, adulation, and fascination as possible. However, her trance was soon broken, along with her heart, when Christian turned around, only to return a sceptical look that gave way to a despicable frown.

'Honey, it looks like you have lost weight. Tell Mama honestly. Did the people at the institute not give you enough food to eat?' Molly asked, hugging his waif of a boy.

Christian didn't reply, his eyes still fixated on his twin, his face still contorted into a frown.

'Molly, is it always the food for you? I mean look at the boy, he is clearly tired from the journey. What say, lad. Do you want to sleep a bit before dinner?' Mr D'Souza asked, patting Christian's shoulder, who still didn't reply but tore his gaze from Christina and silently moved towards the parlour.

'Come, Chrissy, help me out a bit, and let's give your brother some time alone,' said Molly, dragging the former towards the kitchen.

Mr D'Souza took the hint and followed suit.

'Mom, do you think he is upset with me?' whispered Chrissy in the kitchen while helping her mother with the dessert.

'Who? Chris? No...Sweetie, why would you say that?' Mrs D'Souza consoled her daughter with a quick peck on the head.

'Do you think he would still do those things? Maybe he still has an affinity for knife-work...' Chrissy muttered slowly, only to be immediately interrupted by her dad. 'Chrissy, we don't discuss things of the past in this house, all right? Now, go give your brother some company in the living room. I will help Mama with dessert.'

'Ahem!'

Startled by the sudden voice, the three turned around to find Christian standing there.

'Dad, can we go for a walk? It's stuffy inside,' said Christian, in a voice that was all too familiar and, yet unfamiliar, booming with hormones spurting of adolescence.

Christian had finally said something, although still refraining from any eye contact with them. His eyes were glued to the invisible spot on the floor. Nevertheless, the D'Souzas were happy that he had finally broken that unbeknownst vow of silence and had come up with something other than a guttural noise. In fact, it was much more meaningful; it was a request! After so many years their child had requested something, and his wish must be fulfilled.

'Why not, son? What say we reignite our Christmas tradition of picking logs together for the fireplace? Hmm? Let's go!' Ramsay chimed without waiting for Christian's reply, entwining their arms and dragging him towards the backdoor that led to the woods.

Christian accompanied him quietly, shooting another lingering look at his twin. This time something churned in Chrissy's insides. She felt cold beads of perspiration wet her neck despite the wintry month of December.

'Mom, I'll go prepare a warm bath for Dada,' she announced, trying her best to divert her focus from Chris's stiff behaviour while still looking elated.

'I am so glad time hasn't changed the bond you two share. Surely, he'll feel elated to see a comforting, warm bubble bath when he returns,' she told Chrissy while gently squeezing her shoulders with affection.

Chrissy ran upstairs, sneakily wiping a rogue tear from her left eye.

An hour later, Molly was ready with her seven-course meal. She was setting the dinner table when she heard a commotion. It was only when the noise grew into wild lamentation did she go out to check. It was Rani and Patil, their new neighbours, a young couple.

'Aye, Rani, what happened, baba?' Molly asked in her usual motherly manner.

'My baby...my baby, I had just put him in a stroller on the porch, and then it started to get cold and windy, so I thought let me just quickly grab the blanket from inside. I did not even take five minutes, but when I came back...he was gone...gone! Our baby...Why would someone take him, Patil?' she cried, sobbing uncontrollably.

By now, even Molly was stricken with terror, grief, and confusion. She knew that the poor couple had been trying for a baby ever since they moved here, eighteen months ago. But were unable to conceive, despite the best of treatments. It was no less than a miracle of God when four months ago, Rani delivered a premature baby, Ravi. Molly thought back to when Rani had narrated with great pride her journey to Molly, about the former's perseverance through the testing time, keeping faith in the Lord and the Lord finally rewarding Rani with a miracle in the form of Ravi.

Rani's inconsolable crying had garnered the attention of other residents from faraway blocks too. By now, Molly saw her husband and daughter rushing out from the bungalow.

'Ramsay, when did you come back? And where is Christian?' Molly asked aside in a broken whisper.

'He said he was feeling cold...so...' He looked at Molly when realization struck him, making him turn his sentence over. 'You and Chrissy, go inside and check his room. I'll stay here with Rani.'

As Molly accompanied Christina inside, she could hear some of the old residents talking.

'Oh, apparently he is back,' said one.

'Aah, now it will all begin again!' cackled another.

As poor Molly and her daughter ascended the rustic Georgian-style staircase, with each step, the voices from outside became increasingly louder.

And with each step, Molly leaned more and more onto the railing, her frail, old hands gripping the railing tightly as if she feared fainting any moment.

'Mama, are you okay?' Chrissy asked, supporting her mother's heavy frame with her mousy build.

'Yes, child,' the typical mother in Molly spoke, trying to make her child comfortable over easing her own discomfort.

Molly knew now was not the time to fall weak, so she pulled herself together. 'Chrissy, you wait right where you are and keep listening to what the people outside are saying. I will call you if needed.'

'Okay, Mama,' Chrissy nodded like the obedient child she was.

'What are you talking about?' Molly overheard another booming shriek from Patil, as she struggled to reach the last step of the staircase leading to their estranged son's room.

Shunning the voices from outside and those on the inside, she mustered all her courage and tried opening Christian's door. It was jammed. Despite Molly using all her strength, when the door didn't open, she had to call for Christina's help. She came running to her mother's aid and together they opened the door.

If the voices outside were horrifying, the scene inside the room was worse. They saw Christian fidgeting to perfectly secure duct tape on Ravi's mouth. The baby was frantically drumming his little hands in futile gestures of struggle.

'Christian! What have you done?' Molly shrieked but instantly lost her voice on hearing faint sirens in the background. The next thing she heard were some quick footsteps on the staircase outside and, in no time, the door to Christian's room opened with a loud bang.

'My baby...my baby...You psychopath!' Rani shouted.

And with that, Patil and a few other members of the nameless crowd started beating Christian up. Rani retrieved Ravi and removed the duct tape from his tender mouth. While the mother in Molly was crying for her son, she also felt relieved that by God's grace, Rani had Ravi by her side once again.

Once the duct tape was removed, there were two bellowing voices in the room: one was Ravi's frantic cries, and the other was of Christian's pain-filled moans, from the thrashing he was receiving from the fanatical crowd.

'Please...Please stop,' Ramsay gasped, winded after dashing up the hefty flight of stairs despite his years, barely able to control his tears now. The poor father tried to intervene, only to get beaten along with Christian.

'How can they barge into our house like this, Ramsay?' asked a terrified Molly.

'I...I tried to stop them. I even asked them to call the police first, but they didn't hear me,' he said in a defeated voice while still trying to protect his son from beatings.

'Stop it, Ramsay! This is not the first time your psycho son has killed someone. Remember the last time, before your son was sent to the asylum? A couple of gouged bodies of local animals and pets were found in his possession,' said an old man from the crowd.

'I say we kill this demon!' spoke another man, only to be interrupted by a voice on the loudspeaker.

'Step aside, everyone! This is the Vizag Police! We advise you not to meddle with the law.' A young man's voice boomed on the speaker. Accompanying that warning, everyone soon heard the rushed footsteps of the police entering through the main door and hurrying up the staircase. The man with the mouthpiece, Sub-inspector Thambe, pulled out a pair of handcuffs from his pocket and locked Christian's hands behind his back.

Weeping endlessly, Christian was looking helplessly at his mother, who returned the gaze with equal helplessness. Molly could only watch as the young officer grabbed her son by the nape of his neck and dragged him down the stairs.

'Wait, you can't take my brother to prison. He is a minor.' Seeing that the adults were of no help, Chrissy took things into her own hands and ran to the staircase, ahead of the policeman as if trying to block the latter's way.

'Relax, child, we will just be escorting him to the asylum van that is waiting outside,' said Thambe, still dragging Christian towards the stairs.

But Christian's demeanour changed from supplication to violence when, at the last step of the staircase, he saw his twin. The former tried to lunge at the latter. Thankfully, there were more police officers downstairs who successfully shielded Christina from his grip.

As the officers escorted Christian into the asylum van, he took a final look at this house, aware that it would be his last. It was then that his gaze fell upon Christina once more. Smiling to herself, as if she was mentally communicating with him. Christian needed no telepathy to guess what his evil twin must be thinking.

'Papa repeatedly tried to explain to me how sick you were, Dada. Still I would beg for you, to get you one last chance. Of course, they did, eventually...But now they will be forever hesitant. I just have to put up with my boredom now, to keep "our little secret". I hate it, Dada. When you go away, I have to pretend to be the good one...Of course, that is until you come back again,' thought Chrissy, grinning as she grabbed at the duct tape, hidden in her back pocket.

DYBBUK

A demon from Jewish folklore, a dybbuk often clings to antique boxes and objects. But what if it clings to you?

THEY SAY BE CAREFUL WHAT YOU WISH FOR, AND THEY ARE ABSOLUTELY right!

If you see me today in this 2BHK prison that I call my duplex apartment – with no one who visits, no friends, no family – you will be surprised. A lonely, starving, broken man – broken quite literally. You would never believe how and what my life was like, exactly a year ago.

I led a rich life, and I was so full of life. A secure government job at a national bank, which supplied a good salary along with enough time for myself and my family. Family – I had a small but lovely family. My mother lived in the peaceful suburbs on the outskirts of the bustling city of Meerut. We used to visit each other quite frequently. And I used to spend the rest of my time with my beautiful girlfriend. I still cannot fathom how life had blessed me with such a stunning and brilliant woman like her. In all honesty, I never could have foreseen a model developing feelings for me, much less dating me, but Saumya cherished and adored me more than I could have ever imagined.

With these two lovely ladies in my life, everything felt quite fulfilling. As for the remaining time, I enjoyed my me-time. I had a few hobbies – I was a food blogger, a successful one at that. In hindsight, I find it amusing that at one point in time I used to eat and enjoy actual food. Unlike today when I barely eat anything or, worse, eat anything just for sustenance.

It all started last year, in that damned year! My life changed completely. I remember it clearly. It was New Year's Eve, and after spending lavishly on gifts for my girlfriend and renewing my mother's healthcare policy, there was barely anything in my account to purchase something nice for myself.

Rohan, you should really start saving something for yourself, man.

I was in the process of chiding myself for being extravagant on Saumya when a rustic, embroidered, leather journal caught my attention in a worn-out antique shop, which was around the corner on my way home, just two blocks away.

The store manager, a balding man in his seventies or eighties, was about to draw the shutter when I requested that he let me have a look at the tan book on display. He wrinkled his eyebrows in a mixture of contempt and frustration, only to reluctantly lead me inside while mumbling something unintelligible.

The store had numerous pretty trinkets and unique items on display, but I could barely see them in the dim light. Not that I minded, as my thoughts were consumed by the journal displayed on the left window. Boy! It was beautiful to the extent of being mesmerizing, with equally stunning, skin-pale pages made of what seemed like a rare variety of leather.

Something was just so captivating about it, making me unable to hold back from spending a whopping thousand rupees on a hundred-page journal. I was so happy to finally buy something for myself, even if it was a bit overpriced. I instantly made a mental note to use that journal to plan my life better, starting that very day itself.

So, as soon as I reached home, charged by renewed vigour, I flipped to the first page of its leaves. Grabbing my fanciest ink pens, I started charting my resolutions for the new year. And what better day to do that than on New Year's Eve itself.

I was mindful about not going overboard with it, so I stuck to smarter and shorter goals. The top three that came to mind were:

- *I will control my diet and shed some weight.*
- *I will splurge less on my girlfriend and save more.*
- *I will convince my mother to move in here so we can always be together.*

Satisfied with my goals, I signed the date, broke the nib of the pen to mark the finality of my resolve, and went to sleep.

Initially, I was quick to dedicatedly follow and work on all my resolutions. I even lost a few kilos. But as days swiftly passed, I slipped back into my old patterns and the late-night bingeing began.

It was the month of March when the first calamity struck. I was collecting a huge parcel from a food truck. A neighbour's rottweiler, for some odd reason left without a leash, sniffed the air and noticed the chicken wings in my hands, as if confirming with his nose what his eyes had seen. Its fur started bristling with earnest aggression, and it snarled, baring its shiny canines and a salivating tongue. Panic raced through my veins as my latent cynophobia resurfaced.

The dog sprinted towards me. To me, it looked like a mighty soldier charging at me. Petrified, I started running in the direction of my house, darting through narrow alleyways. The sound of claws clicking on the pavement echoed closely behind, growing sharper and louder with every step. My breath came in ragged gasps as I turned a corner and spotted the familiar silhouette of my house in the distance.

With another burst of adrenaline, I pushed my heavy body forward, my footsteps resounding in the quiet night. The dog's bark pierced the air, its determination evident. Fear gripped me once again, urging me on. Blinded by terror, I failed to notice the danger approaching from the opposite direction.

A set of headlights illuminated the path ahead, and a loud honk pierced through the night. Startled, I stumbled as a crack in the pavement caught my foot. The blaring resonance of the horn only added to the cacophony of chaos. Fear gripped me, and my eyes widened as I turned to face the oncoming vehicle, too late to react.

The speeding car, oblivious to my desperation, honked again. The driver's frustration was evident. Trying to leap out of the way, my body succumbed to the paralysis of fear in the split second before impact. The screeching tyres drowned out the dog's barks as the car came crashing into my body, sending me sprawling across the asphalt.

A sickening thud echoed through the night, as pain surged through my body. Bones snapped like dry twigs, and the world spun around me. The car screeched to a halt, and the driver rushed out, panic written all over his eyes.

Neighbours emerged from their homes, drawn by the commotion. The dog, sensing the sudden shift in the atmosphere, slinked into the shadows. As I lay broken and battered on the pavement, the once quiet night was suddenly populated with the blurred, distant wail of sirens, the echoes of a chase gone horribly wrong.

I spent the next few weeks in the city hospital, where a plastic surgeon had to restructure my jaw, which had broken beyond self-healing. The surgery was not only excruciating and costly but also necessitated a liquid diet for the next three months.

Thankfully, despite these circumstances, Saumya did not leave my side, even for a second. Not only did she offer her unwavering emotional and mental support, but she was also glued to my side, efficiently making something healthy and soupy, forcing it down my plastered jaw, even when I had no will to live, let alone eat. She would patiently wait for me to finish the soup, clean the dishes, do the laundry, and even go grocery shopping.

Coming from a typical middle-class family with small town values, I sometimes had my qualms about taking it to the next level with Saumya. I did think sometimes whether a beautiful city girl with a successful career would be willing to take on the responsibilities that will come with marriage. However, I was never surer of the fact that she was the one, as I was then. As these difficult months passed, our bond strengthened, and love blossomed further.

Soon, I was back on my feet, able to finally consume some solids.

Despite the negatives of this episode, I found immense joy in the fact that it strengthened my relationship with my girlfriend and also resulted in significant weight loss during the healing process. To my surprise, thanks to the 'magic' of my enforced liquid diet, I ended up becoming leaner than my initial New Year's goal.

In July, my insurance payout came through, covering all the medical expenses. I was beside myself with happiness, happiness that I had not felt in days. I wasted no time and went straight to Tiffany's online store, where I nearly emptied half of my insurance money to buy an exquisite 2 carat solitaire for my girlfriend. She was the best and I wanted to propose to her with only the best too.

Four days later, on a Sunday afternoon, the ring arrived in bright Tiffany-blue packaging. It was two in the afternoon, which meant that she would be at the gym. So, I wasted no time and drove towards her.

There she was, in her element – suspended from the steel frame, upside down, her body stretched gracefully, curls dangling towards the ground, all sweaty, looking sexy as hell, doing upside-down hangs. I could not believe my stars! This woman was going to be my wife. I simply moved into her line of sight. I didn't even call her name; I didn't need to. She saw me with those sharp, beautiful, and playful eyes, meeting mine even from her inverted position. I got down on one knee, pulled out the bright solitaire from the box, pointing towards her, miming 'Marry me'.

She took a moment to compose herself. Her eyes twinkled before glistening with tears. She didn't scream or laugh but just raised her petite hand and covered her mouth; a reflex, typical of a beauty pageant winner upon an announcement of their name. And then came her excitement. I saw her leg twitch, that excited flick of her foot, and her left ankle slipped. Helpless, I did nothing but see the frenzy in her expression as she instinctively tried to reach out for the bar. But fate itself was conspiring against her. The old machinery gave up with a metallic snap, that resounded through the gym. Saumya's eyes widened as she realized she was about to fall. Time stopped for me. I could see gravity pulling Saumya down in slow motion and then she had barely hit the ground when, in complete juxtaposition, I saw the bar falling onto Saumya's head within a fraction of a second. I wish I could've run like a superhero and stopped that thing in time, but my legs were frozen. My voice choked. My vision had become a blur.

The faulty machinery had collapsed, sending the weighted bar crashing onto her head. A sharp, searing pain shot through her, communicated by her contorted expressions, and a lull fell over the otherwise bustling gym. Everything was still as the clatter of the fallen bar subsided.

And then the gasps from onlookers filled the air as they rushed to Saumya's aid but I stood there shocked beyond measure. My gaze fixed on Saumya as my world had come to a crashing end. Saumya was sprawled on the gym floor, her face contorted in pain. The gravity of the situation reinforced itself as concerned voices murmured around her. Within a split second, all I could see was blood everywhere, and with one last painful sigh, she was gone.

After three months of battling depression, I somehow mustered up the courage to step outside my house. My poor mother, despite her old age, had to come to live with me, and she tended to me all this time. Consumed by a debilitating mixture of overwhelming guilt and a desire to escape, I lost even more weight. I had started resembling a mere skeleton.

Life is funny. I kept thinking during those sleepless nights. *I achieved my goal weight, but at what cost*, I wondered. *I wanted to splurge less on my girlfriend, but at what cost*. And even my resolution to make my mother move in with me...

'Oh shoot!' I yelled as realization dawned on me. 'All those resolutions...It's the diary! It grants wishes but exacts a sinister price for each one it fulfils,' I whispered, finally decoding the puzzle that lay in front of my eyes all this while.

I immediately began scrounging through all my cupboards, looking for to the cursed diary. On finding it, I nervously opened to the only page I had ever scribbled on. Right along the first two resolutions, there were crosses – drawn in what looked like blood-red ink. I had never marked these. My heart sank! Clinging to any and every iota of patience that I had in me, I waited till 10 a.m. the next morning.

I rushed to the antique shop for some answers.

'These things...sometimes these old antique things... carry curses, and evil attaches itself to them,' said the old shopkeeper in a surprisingly composed voice, as if this was a usual occurrence at his godforsaken store.

'I don't know about this diary specifically,' he continued, 'but based on my experiences with such things, I would advise you against trying to burn or tear it in vain. It will only enrage the evil further. It's best to keep it where no one else can get their hands on it.' The old man said this while maintaining his composure.

When I returned, I followed his advice to the letter and locked the diary in an old trunk in my attic. I had decided that my mother needed to leave this mess before evil could befall her.

'But you haven't even regained your health, beta! Do you expect me to leave you just like that?' My mother's voice was filled with concern.

'Maa, I told you, I need some time alone. Besides, you've been here for almost three months now. You should go to check on our ancestral house. You can always come back post-Diwali…Being there, you would be able to do the Diwali puja at home,' I said in a soft but firm tone, leaving no room for negotiation.

'Hmm okay, if you really want me gone, then I will leave,' she replied with mock anger and traces of hurt, which I chose to ignore.

Without wasting another breath, my mother started packing right away. While I started looking for the most convenient Volvo options for her journey back. By nightfall, she had left, and I was on my own once more.

A few days passed after my mother left. In her absence, my mind was occupied in an analysis of the events of the past year, starting from the moment I had purchased that fateful diary.

Everything was fine as long as I maintained my diet and stayed committed to my resolution of losing weight. However, the moment I started slipping back into my old eating patterns, I had the accident that left me on a liquid diet. Similarly, I had run out of my savings, so I, naturally, couldn't splurge on Saumya. But the moment my insurance money came, the first thing I purchased was another indulgence: a ring for her. It was then that the fateful incident at the gym occurred.

Thus, whenever I try or even accidentally stray away from my resolve, the diary takes charge. By the time I finally decoded these patterns, it was Diwali day.

A thought clicked in my mind – the final piece of the puzzle – my mother had moved in with me like I had wanted, but I had made her leave. In trying to protect her, I realized that I had instead put her at risk. I had to get her back home before the diary took charge of the situation in its own twisted ways.

Without another thought, I jumped into my car, hoping that Diwali celebrations would ensure lighter traffic on the road. I put my foot a little too hard on the accelerator, speeding the car into motion. In my heart, I pledged to stop only after reaching my mother's door.

My estimate was right. It usually takes me four hours to reach our hometown, but that day I entered the locality in just two. I was only a block away from her house.

The town was ill-lit, unlike metro cities, with only a few long-fused light poles that had seen better days. It was also a little late at night, and all the shops were already closed. Thus, as a result of my nerves and confusion, I took the wrong turn. But almost immediately, I realized my mistake and started to reverse my car. Unfortunately, the rear-view camera wasn't working, and I didn't notice the woman crossing the street at the same time I was taking the reverse turn.

Boom! I heard my car hit the person's fragile bones.

My conscience nudged me to get off and help the poor woman who was struggling in pain, but I was so scared that I fled the scene.

Back at my house at four in the morning, I crashed on the main porch, exhausted by a mixture of fear and tiredness. Later, around 8 a.m., I decided to go take a look at my car. There were some streaks of blood on the tyres, but nothing else. I started washing and scrubbing the tyres very carefully and was eventually able to get rid of all the red stains.

When I was done cleaning my car, around 10 a.m., I received a call from the Meerut police station informing me that some drunkards had run over my mother last night, just a block away from her house. The police could not identify the car as it was too dark, and the CCTV cameras weren't working. They were bringing the remains here, to hand them over to me, her direct family, for the final rituals.

It felt as if my soul had left and abandoned my body, leaving me hollow and numb. I cried and cried the whole night after her body arrived. I resolved not to cremate my mother. Instead, I chose to lay her to rest in the sanctuary of our backyard, where she could be close to me forever. Thus, we could be together forever, like I had stated in that wretched diary.

My friends – the few I was left with – couldn't comprehend or concur with my decision to bury her. But they grasped that the sequence of unfavourable occurrences over the course of this year had undoubtedly made me a little cuckoo in the head. Understanding my altered state of mind, they refrained from probing further or challenging my decisions.

Exactly one year has passed since the ill-fated purchase of that diary, marking another 31 December since my life turned topsy-turvy.

But I can't continue any longer, living with the guilt that because of me, both my mother and Saumya died such painful deaths. Therefore, I have made the decisive choice to end my suffering and reunite with my loved ones in what I hope is a peaceful afterlife.

To anyone reading this journal, heed my warning: steer clear of antique items, for you never know what you might inadvertently invite into your life.

JORŌGUMO

A spider woman from Japanese folklore, a Jorōgumo manipulates small, fire-breathing spiders. What happens when folklore no longer stays confined in books and starts weaving itself into your life?

HE WOKE UP TO THE HUGE, INSECT-LIKE CREATURES LOOMING OVER his bed, and screamed his lungs out.

'Wait... Is this a nightmare again, or is it for real?' Danuj tried to reassure himself. 'I wonder if men can identify signs of insanity within themselves.'

'Sometimes I think that my brain is unable to hold itself together. It is overflowing with horror... There is no one. No one for me to rely on. I have never been so completely alone. I think I am poisoned. I cannot sleep, nor close my eyes without seeing those damned spiders,' mumbled Danuj for what seemed like the nth time this week.

If only it had been a nightmare, something to laugh over; a festering imagination.

With each passing day, it is becoming increasingly difficult to tell the difference between a nightmare and reality. When the lights fade and the moon rises, anything can happen, as the world becomes a darker place; literally and figuratively. Every twilight, when the sun sets, Danuj contemplates sleeping, but then thinks he might just end up stuck in another nightmare. So he waits until exhaustion takes over his body and puts him to sleep involuntarily.

Life had not been easy for Danuj ever since the pandemic struck. Losing his parents to COVID-19 made him shift from the heart of the bustling metropolitan area of Mumbai to the sleepy suburb of Lonavala. He wasn't always the recluse that COVID-19 and grief-induced depression had shaped him into. He no longer desired the city lights, inclined towards building a peaceful life within the secure boundaries of his home. The new Lonavala accommodation provided him with the silver lining of ample space, a rarity in the city. However, the recent nightmare of an infestation of thousands of spiders in his house, invading his room, only to disappear as soon as he opened his eyes, hindered the pleasure he accrued from the only comfort he had.

Having no one to share his woes and concerns with, Danuj couldn't sleep a wink, shaking and tossing in bed to keep nightmares at bay (or for his actual safety? Which of these, he wasn't sure of). Days, however, were usually good or 'normal', until they weren't.

It happened one morning, and simultaneously things started falling apart for him rather than falling into place. Spiders were no longer limited to his nightmares as he would often see them crawling in the corners between the walls, falling in his meals, or peeping from inside his pillows in broad daylight. No amount of pest control helped.

On a wet, lonely night, there was a tap on the door of the attic, which he had never explored since moving in. Gathering his courage, Danuj climbed the ladder and opened the door to the top. What he saw next was surreal, almost dystopic; it terrified but did not scare him, for he was beyond bewilderment now.

Thousands and thousands of spiders were roaming around and seemed to be casually chatting as if in a social gathering. In one corner, they were even cooking something in an old vessel. As much as Danuj was terrified, he was also enjoying this surreal show. These tiny creatures magically moving around objects three times their size as if it were nothing. One of them, 'the creatures', saw Danuj spying on them. But instead of feeling annoyed, the creature gently pushed a plate filled with whatever stuff was in the old vessel towards Danuj before retreating to a safe distance. Danuj felt as though it was some kind of initiation ritual, as if the creatures wanted him to be a part of their cult. Hesitantly, he accepted the gift, peace treaty, or whatever the dish was supposed to be. The creatures chittered excitedly.

This happened every day for weeks. At first, he was worried thinking that they might be poisoning him; especially after a particularly greasy breakfast that left him clutching his chest from heartburn. As a result, they replaced his meals with fresh fruits, salad and soup. Danuj was instantly grateful for their geniality towards him.

This camaraderie continued to grow day by day, and things escalated beyond just dinner invitations. The spiders now drew hot, steamy baths for him, making him relax at once after an exhausting work-from-home shift.

A few more days passed with this routine, and the rain was now replaced by chilly breezes and long wintry nights. The spiders continued their hospitality, so much so that they even started tucking Danuj into bed with a warm wool-like blanket that they had woven themselves for their guest. It was bizarre, but, as mentioned before, Danuj was beyond bewilderment now.

One such night, Danuj's trance-like sleep was broken when he heard screams from downstairs. He raced to find a decapitated man being devoured by these 'creatures' – insects, spiders, or whatever the hell they actually were.

He was sickened to the core at the sight in front of him, instantly thinking of the mistake he had made in trusting them as friends when they were actually potential foes. But then, he noticed a gun in the man's hand, and realized that he was, in fact, a burglar who had broken into his house. The creatures had saved him, proving once again that they were indeed his friends.

Embarrassed about doubting his friends' intent, he helped the spiders dispose of the mortal remains of the intruder the best he could.

Soon came a morning when the creatures wouldn't let him leave his room. Luckily, it was a holiday. Danuj lay there, confused but yielding, as they ushered him back into bed.

'Maybe they want me to rest a bit extra on a Sunday. Hell yeah, I deserve some rest!' he mumbled.

Hours later, his sleep was broken with a sharp stinging pain searing through his body. It felt like his stomach was filled with razor wires.

He felt a terrible squirm underneath his skin. In a split second, he noticed his stomach splitting open and thousands of 'creatures' making their way out of it into this material world. The insects chittered as he spasmed and moaned. As he was dying and shrieking with agony, he heard the 'creatures' chirping with joy one last time. He instantly realized that the spiders were never trying to protect him. All this while, they had been tending to their young ones inside him.

ZOMBIES

A Haitian mythological undead creature that is created when a corpse gets reanimated. So, what happens if these corpses leave their graves and walk into your life? Guess what? The dead do come back!

'GITA, A 700-VERSE HINDU SCRIPTURE IN SANSKRIT, HAS enlightened mankind about righteousness, dharma, and *moksha*. This eternal message of spiritual wisdom from ancient India is thus called the "Song of God". This is Pradeep, and you are listening to my podcast *Pondicherry Nighttime*,' said the podcaster before cueing in another transcendental song.

That time was a series of many firsts for me. My first trip to India was to the White Town of Pondicherry, also known as mini-France; France is my homeland – a place I would probably never see again. It was also the first time that I heard the prophecy from a holy Hindu scripture, the Bhagavad Gita, on the podcast. The speaker mentioned how the prophecies from the text about the present age of Kaliyuga resonate with the current state of society, emphasizing the prevalence of corruption and superficiality in today's world.

Honestly, I had no interest in religion whatsoever. I only tuned in to that podcast because someone told me that the guy occasionally played good transcendental music. And at that point, I was missing trance, which is a genre that not many stations play in India. It's amazing how this one station stood out from the rest. After all, music transcends borders and always reaches a global audience.

Incidentally, it was also on that podcast that I first heard of 'them', something I didn't know would spread to the entire world so quickly.

'Those who have thoroughly read the Bhagavad Gita will be aware that in the last section is a list of prophecies for Kaliyuga, the present age,' the man continued after the music had ended. 'Kaliyuga is marked by widespread corruption and malice, where people only have a very superficial idea of what it means to live a good, meaningful life.'

'This sounds like our present situation.' I snorted as the man spoke in the background.

'The peak of this dark age will make people extremely intolerant and violent. Even their belief in God will die out. Harassed by famine and excessive taxes, people will resort to eating leaves, roots and human flesh...The streets will turn even more congested, with no space to drive and no place to walk. They will be everywhere,' said the podcaster. That piqued my interest. What did he mean by 'they'? I thought to myself. However, the speaker had already moved on and ended with the last song of the day.

'Anyway, those who have read the holy book say we are apparently still in the middle phase of Kaliyuga, and there is still some time until we reach the tipping point,' were the podcaster's last words that night.

Haunted by the words of the podcaster, I conducted a quick internet research of my own and turns out these prophecies are not found in the Gita alone, the Kalki Purana also mentions that at the very end of Kaliyuga, the ultimate incarnation of Vishnu – Kalki – will take birth. With the aid of the Chiranjeevis, the immortal souls who survive through every age, he will destroy the Kali demon, which by then will dwell in the hearts of humankind itself. That destruction will not only mark the end of this age, but will cleanse the world, ushering in the light of Satyuga once again – a new beginning where truth reigns supreme.

To live is to betray, but why does life itself have to betray us? The betrayal that is the universal downfall in Kaliyuga arrived sooner than we had anticipated. In March 2020, the Indian government, along with the rest of the world, imposed a lockdown due to a deadly virus, leaving me stranded in Pondicherry.

Pondicherry Nighttime served as my solitary source of relief during a period of extreme distress for me, lasting until May 2020. On one such night, at 12 a.m., the only thing that was beating the humdrum of this sleepy town was my favourite late-night podcast. I had formed a weird camaraderie with this man; his voice would not only soothe me but also provide a warm hope.

However, that night, I heard him pause in the middle of a sentence, followed by a faint stammer and then a full-blown wail.

'What the hell is that, guys? Can you see it from your windows too? Look up at the sky, everyone! It's shooting, spitting something that looks like fireballs? Humans? Aliens?

Are we being attacked, oh? Oh my god, oh, oh, not another disaster amidst this pandemic!' said the podcaster, which was followed by a long machine beep.

My heart raced as I listened to the panic in his voice. I quickly ran to the window and looked up at the dark blue expanse, only to see bright flashes of light streaking across the darkness. My mind raced with fear and confusion – was this really happening? Were we being attacked by some foreign government? Or was it the extraterrestrials? I sat frozen in front of my window, waiting for more information, but all I could hear was the eerie silence left by the podcaster's now-silent voice.

I never heard his voice again, but in the next few days, what he had said began to make sense.

They were everywhere – on the streets, on pavements, in front of your main porch – crowding the routes that, thanks to the pandemic, had turned vacant. You couldn't drive or move without colliding with them. Aimless, incoherent beings roamed everywhere with blank faces and empty eyes. They had pale white, withered skin, blue hollows in their bones, and bruised eyes. Their numbers kept growing exponentially every day.

And it was not just Pondicherry; it was Delhi, Mumbai, Dhaka, Karachi, Manila, London, Washington, Paris and all over. It was a global phenomenon; every news channel that had been preoccupied with COVID-19, was now reporting various incidents and theories about this new phenomenon.

A full-page article on the front page of the *Chennai Times* read, 'The streets are now lined with the undead, their hollow eyes and decaying flesh showing a stark contrast to life arrested inside the houses. People are scared, seeking shelter wherever they can find it. But there is no escaping these "undead". The end is near, and our once bustling metropolis is now a graveyard of lost souls. Looking at the chaos unfolding, one wonders, if this is the end to the beginning or the beginning of the end; the final chapter in the story of humanity's downfall.'

You could see them on the newsflashes: masses and masses of people moving in every direction, as if there were billions of patches of skin moving around aimlessly. In fact, never on television or in real life have I ever seen such a sea of people dominating the road!

Politicians say it is a new virus – a bioweapon. Sceptics say it is an alien invasion. The religious say it is doom – the apocalypse, Judgment Day, has arrived.

Whatever it was, one thing was clear: the 'dead' were dropping from the skies like incessant rain all around the world. One could guess that with crime at its peak, hell was full, and the dead had nowhere to go but to fall back to the earth.

The media also extensively covered reports and ran stories from witnesses about how some of 'them', the undead, approached their former homes, where they used to live when they were alive. They would stand outside their former homes, staring blankly at the space, as if trying to establish some connection with their previous lives. Most of the relatives who appeared in the news interviews said they either shouted in horror, cried or even fainted upon seeing their once beloved kin like 'this creature' that looks outright demonic.

Interestingly, these people didn't rise from graves. It was like souls falling from the skies (are angelic heaven and hellish creatures alike?). Therefore, the incident was not attributed or claimed by any specific religion. Some of the people who had returned were already cremated, and their ashes were dispersed in the holy Ganga; or claimed, as per their faith, by their family members.

Funny – that's what I think of this whole situation. Especially because all of us, at one point in time, have wished for a close and dear one to return from the dead with earnest grief and longing. Until they actually do, and then it's a sight of sheer repulsion. And these people, 'the loved ones', no one wants them anymore. Well, such is life, each day the bar is set low and lower for humanity.

Alas! This reminded me of the impending peak of Kaliyuga.

'They' were not harmful per se but chaotic nonetheless. Or maybe, as the podcaster had said, it was only a matter of time till the Kaliyuga reaches its penultimate moment and man turns to eating another man, wiping out the human race. Who knows when that will happen!

Will Kalki arise along with the Chiranjeevis or the immortals. Or wait! Have the immortals (undead) already arrived?

GHOUL

A demon-like being or monstrous humanoid originating in Arabic folklore, a ghoul is often described as a hideous creature who possesses you or shapeshifts to appear alluring enough to lure you easily.

THERE WAS A TIME, LONG AGO, WHEN I USED TO BE A LADIES' MAN. ALL I had to do was point at a woman, and she would allow me to part her legs to kiss the juncture like I was drinking from the honey pot of heaven, inhaling her salty scent and feeling the iron in her veins. I thought I knew at least something about being a Casanova.

To me, in this cruel, scheming city, lovemaking was like creating one's own magic. Magic to fulfil desires and to get through the desperate hustle of staying alive every day. Especially in times that were preoccupied by desperation and hunger, I would take sporadic long drives to the suburbs. The empty streets and silent houses served as the perfect backdrop for my illicit encounters, adding fuel to my insatiable appetite for passion and pleasure. Each rendezvous was like a breath of fresh air, a temporary escape from the harsh reality of my existence. But deep down, I knew that this series of fleeting moments of ecstasy was just a futile Band-Aid, against the deep cut of emptiness that consumed me – just a hollow attempt to fill the void within my soul.

As I would drive aimlessly through the night, chasing after the next thrill, I yearned for a connection that went beyond physical desire, something that would truly fulfil me. But as the city lights blurred past my window, I couldn't shake the feeling of loneliness that lingered within the depths of my heart. Was I destined to just wander throughout my life, searching for something that may never truly exist? The thought weighed heavily on my mind.

I was grateful that it was the weekend once again, so I decided to bid a temporary adieu to the rusted cogs of the godforsaken city machinery. I raced down the dark, empty streets with nothing but the hum of my car engine and the echo of my own thoughts. Little did I know that this ride would take a twisted turn into bad dreams and lost love.

I was whooshing past the almost deserted highway of Kashedi Ghat, also known as the Mumbai–Goa Highway. A cool wind blew through my hair. A sweet smell of the lady of the night rises through the air. Up ahead in the distance, I saw a shimmering neon sign. Tired from driving the entire day, my head grew heavy, and my sight dimmed. I had to stop for the night.

As I stopped in front of a hotel, bathing in pink flamingo light, I saw her standing in the doorway.

I heard the mission bell, and I was thinking to myself, 'This could be heaven, or this could be hell.'

As she led the way, I followed her upstairs in a trance. I thought I heard some voices down the corridor asking me to run away.

'Welcome to the Hotel Infintia,' said the pretty receptionist, white as the colour of milk, as she handed me the keys to my room.

'It's a lovely place,' she continued as she showed me the insides of the room.

'What a lovely face,' I said in my head, disinterested in the room and more interested in her ivory flesh.

'Plenty of rooms at the Hotel Infintia, any time of year. You can find it here.' She continued with what seemed like the marketing jingle of the deserted hotel.

As I saw her leave the room, I noticed the gems she wore; they were much more than she could ever afford. 'Her mind is Tiffany-twisted,' is what I concluded with a coy smile.

My eyes followed her to the courtyard, where she found herself with a lot of pretty boys. I assume she calls them 'friends'. Oh! How they dance in the courtyard.

'Sweet summer swell. Some dance to remember. Some dance to forget.' I hummed the iconic song 'Hotel California' that suddenly popped into my head.

Hopeful for a chance, I called up room service. 'Could you please bring me a glass of wine?'

He said, 'We haven't had that spirit here since 1969.'

'And here I was thinking that I would've had the time of my life.' Dejected at the instant dismissal, I called it a night.

And those voices were still calling me from behind. I woke up in the middle of the night, just to hear them say, 'Welcome to the Hotel Infintia. Such a lovely place.' 'Livin' it up at the Hotel Infintia. What a nice surprise.' 'Bring your alibis.'

I opened my eyes to the exquisite Gothic stained-glass mirrors interestingly adorning the ceiling of this cheap hotel. But what is weirder is that I could see an unnatural version of myself in the ceiling, smiling back at me creepily. The creepy me-but-not-me points to the red liquid oozing from the ice in the stainless-steel ice bucket placed on the mahogany table in the center of the room. Which is strange because I don't recall drinking alcohol. Rather I had called it a night when the restaurant denied having my choice of wine, hadn't I ...?

Then I saw her – no, her reflection – the pretty receptionist, and I thought I heard her say, 'We are all just prisoners here of our own minds.'

As if compelled by a hex unknown, I dragged myself from the only comforting thing in the room – the bed – and followed her apparition to enter what seemed like a master room where they were all gathered for a feast. They stabbed something with their steely knives; to me, it looked like a human thigh.

Held by the hypnotic trance, I watched with what felt like shameless fascination as the knife slid into the flesh with a single smooth swipe and came out with equal swiftness. The knife's metal glistened with a vivid red hue. On its sharp tip was a thick blob, darker than the rest, and a solid-looking piece of meat – meat that was made to cease to live or breathe. This is what broke my trance, and high-pitched scream escaped my mouth, jerking me out of my state.

The last thing I remember is running for my life. I struggled to find the passage as I saw her one more time.

'Relax,' said the pretty waif. 'We are programmed to only receive guests. They can check in any time they like but can never leave.' As she bared her canines under the glaring red lights, I found it difficult to breathe as someone was sucking the soul out of my life. I knew at that moment that this was not a temporary stop for me but a permanent residence, perhaps for eons now.

The creatures of the tribe welcomed me with open arms, their eyes glowing with a mixture of curiosity and hunger. I soon realized that I was not the only one who had fallen victim to this eternal hotel. We were all trapped here, bound by some unknown force that kept us from ever leaving.

As the days turned into years, I found solace in the familiarity of my new companions, knowing that we were all in this together. And so, I resigned myself to my fate, embracing my new life in the Infintia, where time stood still and escape was impossible.

This is all I remember of my previous life before I became part of the tribe. I live here with them, and with all the voices, you would also hear mine.

Welcome to the Hotel Infintia, such a lovely place.

SHAKCHUNNI

The ghost of a married woman, as per Bangladeshi folklore, a Shakchunni lives atop a tree, craving to meet a partner. She also possesses bodies of young brides! But what condemned her to this fate?

THE WOMAN IS A MOUND OF DIRT AND RAGS. A WITHERED RED TANT saree – I don't know if it is red or if the fabric is soaked in blood? Well, people claimed that she reeked of blood!

Almost all residents of Mukherjee Park, the so-called upscale neighbourhood of Kolkata, have seen her at least once. They say that she moves with a lumpy, plodding gait, slowly dragging forward, as if swept by an invisible push. Her long, greasy hair hide her face, but the smeared kajal and grubby lipstick on a once beautiful face still peak through her tresses. The beautiful red and white bangles or the *shankha pola*, worn by married Bangla women, timelessly adorning her frail hands, would jingle as she moved, indicating her arrival to the people of the locality. She is said to disappear in the last leg of the night or in the wee hours of the morning, taking a turn at the end of the lane that would pave the way to the uphill Rai Mansion.

Nobody knows where she goes or what she does during those hours, but rumours of her identity as a ghost or a witch have been established throughout the community. Some say she is searching for her lost lover, while others claim she is cursed to wander the streets forever. Regardless of the truth, the sight of her strolling through the ill-lit streets sends a chill down the spines of those who do cross her path. Her presence is haunting yet mesmerizing, leaving a sense of unease in the air even long after she has vanished into the night.

Some people have cooked up stories with claims that this woman would ring the bell of a random house asking for *mach-jhol*. Whether you accept her request or deny it, either way you're doomed because she will take the life of a loved one soon. Her mere presence is an omen of impending doom. The best you can do is not open the door around those hours and pray to whichever deity you believe in to have mercy and protect you.

This urban legend started when Madhov Da of bungalow number 49, heard a soft knock on his door around midnight five months ago. He saw a mysterious woman asking for *mach-jhol*. Despite feeling unsettled, he denied her request and watched her disappear into the night. The next day brought news that his sister had unexpectedly passed away. Following suit, other residents started attributing any and every unexpected misery that befell them to the supposed Shakchunni.

In the coming days, fear reached its zenith. In order to avoid any ominous encounters, some residents of Mukherjee Park started writing phrases on the main gate, saying 'NOT AT HOME' with holy turmeric and vermillion.

To me, it was still most likely just a superstition or an urban legend. I had never believed in this lore until the fateful day when I was returning from a wedding in a nearby town. Unfortunately, I had to cross the dreaded Rai Mansion to enter Mukherjee Park Road. In the wee hours of the morning, I saw her, and she did look exactly like all residents usually described her. It was even more peculiar to see her suddenly vanish within the boundaries of Rai's mansion.

This piqued the writer's curiosity in me; I now had to find the point of genesis of this situation and, with that thought, I slowly put the ignition to sleep but didn't kill the headlights of my car. I slowly stepped out of my car and started moving towards the mansion's gate. Neither the tales of horror about the dreaded Rai Mansion, nor any impending consequences of trespassing could stop me from climbing the gate to the lawn inside.

Certain houses, just like certain people, are evil. The scent of the ill intentions and deeds committed in such houses is so strong and persistent that it stays even long after the actual doers pass away. The realization that I was standing in such a house made the hair on my neck rise; my body was covered with cold goosebumps.

The dilapidated, haunting appearance of the mansion didn't help to ease my doubts either. It was not just unclean, but hideous, with frayed grass everywhere. I fumbled with my steps as I couldn't see anything, and the ground felt as if covered in carnivorous grass from gory horror movies, which would engulf me at any moment and not even burp.

Using all of my senses, I somehow managed to stumble and reach the porch, when a rodent came running from its hiding place, grazing my foot in the process. The rubbery skin of the rodent left me with tingling nerves, as though my skin were creeping from inside. Terror-stricken, the blood in my veins froze, anticipating what might happen next.

I opened the rotten wooden door to the parlour, and a stench of probably the devil himself dominated my nose. However, the smell was nothing in comparison to what I saw next.

I saw him, Diwan Rai Sahib, the man, the legend himself, whom the people of Mukherjee Park believe disappeared over fifty years ago.

All the stories I had heard since childhood from my relatives or neighbours came flooding back to me.

The legend goes like this: Rai Sahib, in his early forties, married a beautiful woman, who was in her late twenties, from a nearby suburb. Despite being at least fifteen years younger than Rai Sahib, she was of a considerable age, according to the standards society held for women back then. Some people even say that she had a suitor somewhere else too, who was not from an aristocratic caste. As a result, her father gave a hefty dowry and part of his fortune to Rai Sahib for accepting his daughter, as the latter was in great debt. However, this didn't end well, as the girl arguably eloped with her suitor a few months after the wedding. This brought Rai Sahib such embarrassment that, within months of his wife's elopement, he transformed into a prominent drunkard; he stopped meeting people, attending events, until one day he simply vanished. Some go so far as to claim that he drowned himself in the

Hooghly. Although the truth remains that no one has seen him in a long time.

Despite only knowing him as a local legend and never having seen even a portrait, I was certain that the man sitting in front of me was indeed him. With his unkempt beard, probably as rogue and filthy as the grass on the verandah, my gut told me that it was him. On cue, my intuition was verified when I saw a portrait, tilted on a frail wall behind, which had an aristocratic man standing in a royal Bengali *poshak*, twisting his heavy moustache. At the bottom of the painting, in cursive Bangla it read 'Diwan Bhisom Rai Sahib, March 1970'. As the young rays of the dawn wafted in, I could match the unique set of fiery blue eyes on this man's sunken face to the ones on the portrait behind him. There was no scope for doubt, it was Rai Sahib.

It was then that he saw me and smiled, as if he had anticipated my arrival and was waiting for me. 'Come in, Writer Babu,' he said in broken syllables with a hoarse voice, which was a little difficult to comprehend. But like I said before, I knew that this man was waiting for me, waiting to add his side of the story to the legend.

Rai Sahib began narrating the story of his life and how it bore similarities to his favourite poem of all time, 'The Rime of the Ancient Mariner', which he had read a long time ago, perhaps in his childhood. The poem very dramatically illustrates how the consequences of one's bad actions and their guilt never leave them. This burden continues to hang around one's neck like a dead albatross (curse) forever.

Once he was done narrating his story, I found myself trembling, shocked to have realized how we had missed something that had been apparent for so long. Nevertheless, the irony of it was not lost on me.

Now, of all times, he remembered the moral of Coleridge's poem. For fifty years now, every night, he is tied down to his bed, where his dead wife makes love to him in the same stinking *shaadi ka jora* that she was murdered in. The wife, no one in the neighbourhood really saw but only heard the tales of, when she ran away on her very wedding night itself; the woman people now knew as the bad-omen lady.

If only he had remembered the lesson when he was planning to murder his wife for her inheritance, he wouldn't have to go through this agony every night, even after his death. For him, it was his punishment, but for his hopelessly romantic and now-deceased wife, it was the life she had always dreamed of in their beloved Rai Mansion – their happily ever after.

I don't remember much after listening to the tale of gut-wrenching marital horror.

I do vaguely remember some of the words and bits and pieces of sentences like:

'Of course, it was not my child that she was pregnant with.'

'I cursed myself for marrying her but then I remembered about her inheritance as she was the sole heir to her father.'

'But I should have cremated her after poisoning her instead of burying her unceremoniously in the backyard, maybe then she wouldn't have haunted me.'

I am not even sure if I really heard these straight from the horse's mouth, because a passerby had found me the next day, passed out in my car seat. To be honest, I can't even be sure if what I had experienced was anything more than a vivid dream triggered by my curiosity. In fact, I don't think I have the strength to go inside the Rai Mansion again to verify the same. But whether truth or figment of my imagination, all I know is that I now have my next story.

As I sit here trying to make sense of it all, I can't shake the feeling that there is more to the mansion than meets the eye. The chilling details of the story I had heard haunt me till date but despite my fear, the writer in me urges to delve deeper into the mysteries of the Rai Mansion and bring the truth to light. However, there is a solitary sane voice in my head that keeps cautioning me, reminding me that I might not be lucky enough to escape the next time.

CHUPACABRA

A mythical animal from Spanish folklore that sucks the blood from animals, and sometimes from humans too...

THE SCENE ON THE FIELD WAS AKIN TO A MASSACRE. THE SWINE WERE mutilated, and their blood was dripping from the intestines that were splattered everywhere. Given that it was the eve of 31 October, and a scarecrow too was missing from Zakir's cornfield, someone unaware of what had been happening with Zakir for the past six months would've described this eerie event as spooky Halloween lore coming to life. Zakir, however, knew better than that. It was Yama; it had returned from the dead.

It all began six months ago. In fact, all of it began two years ago, when he first encountered it at the renowned Sonepur livestock fair. Zakir had gone there to buy some cattle in bulk for his cornfield, and what was better than Sonepur cattle at wholesale prices? The fair was filled with domestic animals of all sorts, from sheep to camels. There were even wide varieties of watchdogs for farms. And different vendors from different states were offering different prices for all of these. It was ultimately up to one's skillful bargaining to secure the best deal.

Busy negotiating one such deal, Zakir felt something poke him in the back. He turned around only to find Yama staring back at him, the prettiest female kid that he had ever seen. It was so cute, and its eyes were so innocent that it felt treacherous to get mad at them. Those sparkly eyes had the power to make anyone fall in love with them, right at first sight, and Zakir was no exception. He looked around for its owner but found no one selling goats within the radius.

'Let it be. I don't need a goat anyway,' he said to himself, but the little furry thing kept following him around. And just like that he thought, who was he to refuse such affection. As a result, ever since, the goat became part of Zakir's family.

Initially, it was everyone's pet; whether it was Zakir, his wife Roza, or their children, everyone loved this beautiful, luxurious soft-coated goat. The children named it Yama after the beautiful, grey dwarf planet Pluto. Heavier and larger than usual goats, Yama used to trot around and follow Zakir everywhere in the house, making a sweet jingle from the collar bell around its neck. The goat's presence brought joy and laughter to Zakir's household, becoming a beloved companion to all. It was always by his side, whether he was working in the fields or relaxing in the shade. The bond between Zakir and the goat grew stronger with each passing day, and soon, he couldn't imagine life without his loyal and loving friend. The goat had found its forever home, and Zakir was grateful for the unexpected gift of companionship.

But like they say, good times don't last for long. Then came the great Bengal famine, and Zakir started to lose both his crops and cattle to the famine. He wasn't making much profit with the corn anyway, but things started to go further downhill when he accrued losses due to the debt he had taken from the market. The famine had brought him to the road. Once a respectable merchant, he was now merely making ends meet.

This series of unfortunate events pushed him into drinking and distancing himself from his family. Day by day, his health deteriorated. At the same time, his thriving farm fell into disrepair. The happy home transformed into a place of tension and despair. It seemed as if Zakir had lost everything – his livelihood, his family, and his sense of self.

First, his children would no longer come to earnestly hug their father, when he returned home late at night from the local bar. Even when he tried to reinitiate the ritual, they would simply turn their faces away from him, repulsed by the stench on his breath.

'Bloody rascals! When I was bringing them gifts and chocolates, they loved me. Look at them now!' He slurred in an inebriated voice. As his alcoholism worsened, Zakir's wife, Roza had to take on the burden of managing the farm alone. But without his help, she struggled to keep up with all of the work. The once lush fields now lay barren, a stark reminder of the toll his addiction had taken on their family and livelihood.

Roza, a dedicated, religious woman, started distancing herself from her addict husband and would no longer make love to him, at least willingly – because her unwillingness never stopped Zakir from getting what he wanted. As the days passed, he became increasingly abusive towards her.

Things had escalated to a point where no one at home loved or welcomed him, apart from his beloved pet Yama. Zakir believed that the entire world could turn against him except for Yama who would never leave his side. Until, of course, one day it did – just seven months ago.

It was an exceptionally chilly night that brought the family down with it.

It was past midnight on a cold night despite it being the month of April. A drunk Zakir was returning home from the local bar, stumbling across the empty streets of the already-sleeping town. A bright spring moon silvered the roofs, casting deep shadows. A chilled wind gushed through the trees and owls watched him silently as he passed along. In retrospect, it must have been a premonition of the impending doom. Tired of his financial woes and the consequent dejection, Zakir just wanted a warm meal and an even warmer bed to make him forget the freeze that his luck was experiencing these days.

As soon as he reached home, he reached for Roza, forcing himself on her, going about business as usual. But suddenly something sharp hit him hard in the back with great force. Zakir fumbled and took a moment to regain his balance. He turned around to see a very unusual-looking Yama. As if it held a deep look of disgust for Zakir, with its big, round eyes filled with rage towards him.

Zakir felt something happen to him – as if something twisted within him. He could accept rejection from the entire world but how could he handle it from his beloved pet? With utmost rage, he turned to the poor thing, and dragged it towards a corner of the room. Holding her by her horn, he choked the poor thing with all the power he possessed.

All this happened while Roza just sat on the corner of the bed, too horrified to do anything as she watched the animal struggle until it stopped with its mouth gaping open and eyes ajar, staring into nothingness. It was only when she saw Zakir getting back up on his feet, moving away from the dead animal and casually taking its body to dispose of it, that Roza could let out a sob. She couldn't believe all that she had just witnessed. The cruelty and violence Zakir had displayed made her stomach churn. Roza felt sickness creep to her core as she realized the true nature of the man she had once loved. Tears streamed down her face as she mourned the loss of the helpless creature, knowing that she would never be able to look at Zakir the same way again.

Zakir's downfall began the same night, right as he lit the furnace in the living room and unflinchingly threw the poor thing's body in the furnace. The fire crackled as expected when the lifeless body of the goat went inside. However, something unexpected happened, as the playful fire leapt out of the furnace and engulfed the wooden mantle. Within no time, it spread to the embroidered curtains and the home-knit crochet sofa covers around the mantle. The blaze quickly consumed the entire living room, causing irreparable damage to the cozy home Zakir and Roza had lovingly built together. He stood motionless, watching the flames devour their belongings, totally lost in the moment, as though hooked on his destruction.

It was only when he heard his wife and children struggle with the main door, trying to escape to the porch, that he ran and helped them with the door. He saved them in the nick of time, but their treasured house was irredeemable now.

Zakir sobered up after the fire fiasco, before it got worse. With his senses came the guilt. He would incessantly blabber to himself, 'Intense, unrestrained, and soulless... Yes! you must be soulless, Zakir, to have done what you have done, and this is God's way of getting back at you. You deserve this...All glory to Allah! He is kind and merciful, so he kept your family away from his wrath.' Zakir realized the magnitude of his actions and the irreversible consequences of his cruelty.

'But I was maddened by its indifference. It was not natural. It had always shown me the utmost affection. I was tortured by doubt! Its rejection drove me insane.' Roza witnessed him counter-arguing with himself for hours at length.

Over the next few days, he acknowledged and convinced himself that he had indeed committed a horrible crime by killing innocent Yama, and that the house fire was God's way of avenging the poor soul's life. Little did Zakir know that it was far from true. Payback had just started, and it was not God but the Devil himself who was after him now.

It hadn't even been two months since the fateful night, and they had moved to the outer house and lived with whatever servant staff they could still afford. Zakir's overwhelming feelings of remorse couldn't let him stay away from alcohol for long. And after one such night of debauchery, he returned home and slept next to his wife. However, when he woke up the next morning, the bed beside him was vacant. He stretched his arms out and was about to call Roza for his morning bed tea, when his hand grazed a human foot hanging limp from the ceiling.

Her body was attached to the ceiling. It was his Roza. Things had definitely not been the best between them for the past few months, but she was his beloved wife of fifteen years, the mother of their children. He couldn't bear to see her like this; her eyes popping out, tongue sticking out, and body growing blue as it hung from the ceiling. He couldn't believe what he was seeing and felt his heart shatter into a million pieces.

Zakir ran all conscious details of last night in his head, wondering if he did this to her. Only when he heard faint sirens in the background, he realized that his staff must have witnessed this bizarre and gruesome scene and have reported it to the police. He was in a complete state of shock, unable to comprehend what had happened. and the weight of guilt and sorrow bore down on him. He couldn't shake the feeling that somehow, he was responsible for Roza's death.

As the police arrived, he was sure his end was near. In his mind, he was certain that he himself had hung his late wife in a drunken rage. Zakir was taken into custody for questioning, and he was grateful to Allah that his children were at their grandparent's house for vacations or how would have he faced them? Or worse, could he have harmed them too?

The police, however, soothed his worry a bit when they later declared it a clean case of suicide. The authorities theorized that it happened due to the recent loss of wealth, the family bungalow (most of which came from the dowry money Roza's beloved father had saved for her), and subsequent depression. However, what the police couldn't account for was the speckles of gray animal fur all over Roza's body.

The fact that Zakir's bad luck didn't end there. Instances where an unidentified animal or similar entity attacked his employees and cattle, startled him, making him think that something was seriously wrong. That thing has been the reason for his downfall – his wealth, family, mental health, and now his very last source of earnings, his cattle, all gone.

'Not anymore,' Zakir thought to himself. It is tonight that all of this shall end. Tonight, he will decimate that ugly thing again, this time forever.

With the pledge in mind, he went to his field with a scythe in hand. Like a madman, he shouted the thing's name. Instantly, there in the bright, shining moonlight, he saw it. Like a dead person rising from their grave, it, too, was reincarnated from dust and ashes to end the cursed life of Zakir.

Once the apple of his eyes, its face now appeared vile and possessed. The demonic goat stood tall, its blackened hooves digging into the soft earth, as it let out a bloodcurdling scream. Its eyes glaring red, fuelled by an unholy fire, and its razor-sharp horn gleamed in the moonlight. It had been summoned to this place by the man who had wronged it, and now it was time for revenge. With a sinister grin spreading across its twisted mouth, the demonic goat charged towards Zakir, who stood frozen in fear. The air crackled with an otherworldly energy as the two adversaries prepared to face off in a battle that would determine their fate.

Zakir, terrified beyond words, could only watch as Yama closed the distance between them in an instant. Its powerful legs propelled it forward with incredible swiftness, and its sharp hooves slashed through the air, narrowly missing his face. Zakir dodged, trying desperately to evade the goat's relentless assault. He could feel its hot breath on his neck, and the stench of sulfur and brimstone filled his nostrils.

With a sudden burst of adrenaline, he summoned all his strength and made another desperate attempt to fight back. He swung his scythe wildly, hoping to strike Yama's vulnerable underbelly. But the goat was much quicker than he had anticipated, and it easily sidestepped the clumsy attack. Its single half-broken horn, a reminder of Zakir's evil Karma on that fateful night of Yama's murder, flashed in the moonlight as it charged towards the man once again. Eyes filled with an insatiable hunger for blood and revenge; it shoved the uneven horn in the middle of Zakir's chest.

He fell to the ground, feeling the warm blood pooling around him as his vision blurred with the surge of pain that consumed him. The Yama stood over him triumphantly, its eyes glowing with malevolent glee as it prepared to deliver the final blow. The world began to spin around him and Zakir felt a searing ache that seemed to devoured his very being. He could taste the coppery metallic tang of his own blood within his mouth. The demonic goat, sensing its prey's absolute weakness, pushed for its advantage and lifted him off the ground with its horn. Zakir's body felt weightless and helpless as the demonic goat lifted him higher and higher into the air.

The wind rushed past his ears as he ascended to elevations, the ground below disappearing from his view. The pain in his body was unbearable, but his mind was filled with regret and remorse. How could he let things escalate to this point? As he felt himself lose consciousness, Zakir's last thought was a plea for forgiveness, along with a desperate wish that he had never wronged Yama. Or better yet, he had never brought the thing home.

KAPPA

A water spirit who, according to Japanese mythology, inhabits the bodies of water where it drew its final breath. Beware! Even in the afterlife, these creatures continue to struggle with the fire of vengeance and could even pull you along with them.

THE IRONY OF LIFE IS THAT WE TEND TO TAKE THE MOST MUNDANE things in life for granted, without even considering the possibility of a day when we might obsessively yearn for those same things.

This is me, Rohan. I am twenty-three years old. This my story, and interestingly, I haven't slept for fifteen years now.

As a child, I absolutely despised taking afternoon naps. It was the sole reason for various spats between me and my beloved mother. I was almost allergic to the idea of sleeping in the middle of the day, and it felt like a lot of time was wasted. I would run under the bed and hide in a corner, only for my mother to eventually find me and tuck me in.

Barring that, me and my mother were very close; more so because I was born after ten long years of marriage. I was the only reason why she would tolerate my alcoholic, nuisance-causing father. In fact, she was a dedicated government schoolteacher, shaping and improving the lives of numerous students. Whereas my father never managed to seriously devote himself to anything – he would take on a variety of odd jobs, one after another, only to abandon them after finding a new fancy. There were times when his crazy business ideas costed us all our savings.

Despite my father's irresponsible behaviour, my mother always acted as our small family's steadfast anchor. She was the backbone of our household, balancing her teaching job while taking care of me and, on top of that, dealing with my father's antics. I admired her resilience and determination to make the best out of even a bleak situation. In hindsight, I feel grateful for her unwavering love and support throughout my upbringing.

If I talk about my father's antics on the other hand, one such bizarre idea of his, in the spring of the year 2000, changed our lives forever. He quit his clerical job to start a coffee business. As a result of which we had to shift to Coorg from Bangalore. My mother wasn't the happiest with this shift, because she would have to restart her teaching career in Coorg, from scratch. Nevertheless, she tolerated most of my father's antics, including physical and verbal abuse, out of love for me. She understood how vital having the presence of both the parents meant to me.

At the age of eight, I was oblivious to any of my mother's struggles and eagerly awaited this move. This was also the time I had lost my dear pet, a cat, and I wanted to go somewhere I would not be reminded of its memories every second. Moreover, to me, Coorg was a quaint little hill station, brimming with the possibilities of adventures, in comparison to the boring tech park that Bangalore was. I couldn't wait to explore the lush greenery, go on long walks in the forests, and maybe even spot some wild animals. The very thought of life in a small town where everyone knew each other excited me. I was also looking forward to making lots of new friends.

Thankfully, my mother managed to bag a transfer to Coorg. And since it was a jurisdiction much smaller than Bangalore, she even received a promotion to the post of the school principal – with the added benefit of accommodation.

The memory of going to see that house with Mother before moving in is still fresh in my mind. It was a cozy together house, with a grassy green verandah in the front with a small pond attached to it. Even if old, it was beautiful, to say the least. But the fresh garden, the sparkling pond, and the soothing serenity of the place, especially after the chaotic cacophonies of the city, made our day.

'Maybe your dad is right this time, Rohan. Maybe this house will help us redeem our life and relationships,' Mother said, while her eyes were fixed at the far-off orange sunset. Unaware of the gravity of her words, I blurted out, 'Whatever, I know I am super excited to bathe in the pond every day, Mummy.'

'Haha, of course, you can do that, my *chiklu*.'

The amusement in her voice, quite evident, still rings in my ears, as if she was here, standing next to me.

Soon after shifting, things actually took a turn for the better, at least in the beginning. I'm not so sure about my parents' relationship, as my father would, nevertheless, occasionally, beat my mother. But the sun definitely shined a little brighter for me. You see, I was a city boy who knew about the 'world' more than any of the small-town boys in

Coorg. On top of that, my mother was the school principal, so, naturally, everyone wanted to be in my good books.

When we arrived, the summer vacation had begun, so I had ample time to play and chat with the neighbourhood boys for hours at end. This was when I was first acquainted with the myth of Balaram or colloquially called Ballu: a cryptic urban legend written in blood. Nestled amongst the coffee plantations, this town held a story that had been passed down through generations like a precious family heirloom. An unfortunate tale of a young boy whose spirit roamed the streets during the late hours of the afternoon.

Ballu's father had died in the Indo-China War, leaving the young child at the mercy of his stepmother, Shanta. Staying true to the stereotypes about stepmothers, Shanta too was known to be a cruel and heartless woman. She made Ballu do all the household chores while her own children were pampered and spoiled. Not wanting to have another mouth to feed, Shanta started seeking ways to get rid of Ballu. The opportunity presented itself when she decided to punish Ballu for a simple mistake of taking a nap in the afternoon when he was supposed to man their grocery shop. She kicked him out of the house right away and left him in the woods. To this day, people recount how the poor child had wailed the entire day – crying and bellowing and begging – going from one door to another, requesting the villagers to take him in, or at least give him something to eat. But humanity was under the spell of a deep slumber that day, as not a single person let their heart or the door to their house open to welcome the unfortunate child. And just like that, after a few days, Ballu was found dead. Whether he drowned or if he fell into the lake because his body succumbed to weakness and starvation, no one knew, instead?

Since then, a curse befell all of Coorg: if any child was found snoozing in the afternoon, they would be subjected to Ballu's wrath, which would cause a string of unfortunate events. Shanta's children were the very first victims. Just a few days after Ballu's death, bodies of his half-siblings were found dumped in the well outside their house. A bewildered Shanta kept repeating how it had only been ten minutes after she had put her twins to sleep and then went back to attend the customers at her shop. But when she came back, her twins were gone – they were nowhere to be found, until she found their bodies in the compound well. People say she lost her mind after the tragedy and would roam the streets, seeking God's forgiveness. Until one day, she too disappeared, never to be seen again.

Even after feeling the chills from this tragic story, my initial reaction was that it simply was a superstitious tale or legend passed down through generations, to keep naughty children in check. After hearing this tale, back then, in the true fashion of a city boy, I snubbed off the local children as being too gullible and ignorant.

'Wait a minute...What nonsense! I have roamed the entire town, but there is no lake here.'

'There used to be one, but it dried over the years,' replied one of the boys.

'Yes, and then the officials removed the dried debris and merged the active part with a man-made reservoir,' said another.

'And then they built the government accommodations complex over it,' chimed in the first again.

'Wait, you mean the pond in my backyard?' I asked, surprised as they all nodded in unison and I couldn't help my laughter. 'You mean little Ballu is buried in my backyard?' I guffawed again, thinking how dumb these kids were.

Little did I know that fate had an incredible twist in store for me.

Things soon started to go south for us. My father began incurring major losses in his business again, which made him increasingly abusive at home. Whereas the stress of my mother's new responsibilities as the principal coupled with settling into a new city, were taking a heavy toll on her health. It was no surprise when the house turned into a battlefield, with more quarrels than ever before. But it didn't just stop at that, as all of us started experiencing something weird.

More often than not, Mother would find one of the taps in the bathroom running. Sometimes, Father would hear the sound of flowing water but wouldn't find any source in sight. On one such night, all of us saw wet footprints printed all over the house – on the carpet, on the sofa, even on the wall mantles. But the next morning, we saw them all gone, making us think of the incident as a bad dream.

The graveness of the situation eluded us until two significant events occurred.

The first incident was in April. I was sleeping in my cot when I heard a jingling sound. Recognizing the sound, I woke up in an instant. It was the sound of my cat, René's collar bell. There was no one in the room but I could see wet paw prints scattered all over. So, I followed those prints and the faint jingle flowing in from a distance, tracing which I reached the pond. I don't particularly recall anything that happened during the night, but my mother told me that she found me unconscious in the garden the next morning. When I mentioned the sound of René's collar bell, she was a little taken aback and reminded me that our cat had passed away a year ago. It must be some other cat, she soothed me.

'You miss René even now, my baby, and it is okay; grief doesn't go away even after shifting bases, it takes time,' she had said.

After that incident, for a while, everything went back to its normal course in our house. But that was until the first week of May, when all hell broke.

It was a peculiarly scorching summer afternoon, and my mother had made rich, fluffy appams and dosas drenched in piping ghee, accompanied by a rich, creamy meat stew for lunch. As an immediate after-effect, I felt extremely sleepy. The food coma, coupled with the boredom from the time of the day, lulled me into a deep sleep. Thus, I broke the key condition of the dreaded Ballu urban legend; I fell asleep in the afternoon. I am still unsure whether my memory served me right or if my overactive mind went on overdrive. Nevertheless, all of it continues to haunt me to this day.

In my dream, our house had transformed into an abandoned cottage with cobwebs all over. It looked as if it were a remanent of a bygone era. I gingerly opened the gate to that forgotten house. The dimly lit corridors seemed to close in on me, the musty air thick with unspoken evils. I couldn't help but wonder if I was really prepared for what lay ahead, and whether my courage would be a resource enough to guide me through the darkness.

Then, as if following a whispered invitation in the wind, I stumbled upon it: a glinting bronze pot nestled amongst the cobwebs and dust. With trembling hands, I reached for it, and simultaneously felt a chill run down my spine, as if the air around me had turned into ice. I saw a child, a year or two older than me. Was this Ballu? He pointed towards the pond in the backyard. Feeling like his order was my command, I immediately followed his fingers to note what he was pointing at in the pond, and I couldn't believe my eyes. It was him – the boy! But wait...No! It was his body floating in the pond – before he could say anything, I heard a piercing scream sprawling my eyes open.

I woke up to the horrendous sight of my father dragging my mother by her hair. Her face was battered and bruised. It was peppered with several cuts, and she was bleeding profusely. My mother was crying, screaming, and begging him to stop. Was it another bad dream, or was this actually happening? I wasn't sure. Taking a leap of faith, I went ahead and tugged on the cloth of my father's kurta, asking him to stop hurting my mother. He slapped me instead, which unleashed something in me. Even as an eight-year-old, I still remember what happened vividly.

It felt like it wasn't me, but someone else inside me; as if someone had taken over my body. I don't know how I inadvertently stumbled upon something malevolent, which instantly latched onto me. My body felt sluggish and heavy, yet it was floating at the same time. It was draining my life force.

Pumped by the varied mixture of sensations in my body, I channelled all my energy to strike my father. He leapt in the air and was pushed into the bathroom before falling on the floor, where as if at its own will, the shower started pouring. He was stuck in the bathroom for a long time, shouting as the shower released a torrent of scalding hot water over him. As if held in place by some unseen force, all his attempts to escape failed. Struck with terror, he kept gazing at the toilet seat.

Possibly the same force, or a mixture of fear and pain, kept my mother frozen in her spot. Thus, stopping her from helping my father in any way. But I was the one who ran towards the bathroom, trying to peek through the curtain, just to get a glimpse of the entity that my father was looking at. In hindsight, I wish for a better last memory of my father.

This entity, which most probably was Ballu, had gray skin and only a few patches of long, thin hair on his head. He had nails that were at least a foot long. The nails held a deep red sheen from blood, along with pieces of flesh hanging off their tips. Ballu had an invisible hold of my father's leg, which soon started to blister from the unending onslaught of hot water. I could hear Ballu let out a creaky chuckle as he saw my father struggle. Making a last gurgling call, my father fainted – at least, that's how it appeared to me.

The next thing I knew, I was blacking out. When my eyes opened, my head was on my mother's lap. Two days had passed since that incident. When I enquired about my father, she told me that he died of a heart attack the same day; he couldn't even make it to the hospital. His funeral was short and quick, attended only by his brother. My mother let out a faint smile, trying to assure me that everything would be fine. Little did I know that it was probably the last time I saw her smiling.

I remember little of the days that followed as I didn't really feel like much of myself either. But my relatives say that I had started exhibiting strange and unsettling behaviour. On one such occasion, my mother found me eating a raw crow. It didn't take much more for her to realize that there was something terribly wrong with me, which was probably way beyond the jurisdiction of a doctor. Hence, the same day she took me to a local priest who told her about the legend of Ballu.

'I am a teacher, and I shouldn't be believing all this but when it comes to my child, baba, I am just a mother. There must be something you can do,' my mother had literally begged as per the verbatim.

'I really wish my child, but this entity is beyond my abilities to help you,' the priest had replied.

However, my mother wasn't one to be deterred, she went from pillar to post, mandir to masjid; meeting saints of every religion to administer any relevant ritual possible. Alas! Nothing worked.

Meanwhile, my body was falling apart a little every day, making me weaker with each passing day, so much so that it was an effort to even breathe.

When even faith failed my mother, she decided to take things into her own hands. She actively started researching and collecting information about Ballu. She went so far as to even meet some of his victims' families.

During her research, my mother scraped off all the artifices of the matter, to uncover the realization that Ballu was still just a lost child who simply longed for his mother's love and that's the reason he wasn't able to transit to another realm. That's when it struck her that the only way to save me was if she was willing to give Ballu what he needed the most. There was no way to guarantee her success, but perhaps, if she offered herself as his mother, Ballu might leave me alone and find peace.

Despite her fear and uncertainty, my mom found courage in her motherhood and became drawn to the idea of offering Ballu the love he so desperately sought. With trembling hands, but empowered by her faith in her motherhood, my mother approached his shrine: the pond in our backyard.

Her heart filled with trepidation and compassion, she cried, 'If this is what it takes to save my son, then I must do it.'

She knelt on the ground as if before an altar, a strange sense of calm washing over her. She closed her eyes and took a deep breath, imagining all the love she held for me to expand and engulf the lost, lonely spirit of Ballu. Tears streamed down her face as she offered her heart to the 'malevolent' force, praying that he would find the peace and acceptance he had longed for.

For what seemed like an eternity, there was no response, and my mother feared that her attempt had failed. Until suddenly, warmth spread across her body, as if a weight had been lifted from her shoulders. She opened her eyes to find Ballu's spirit hovering before her, its features softening and its eyes now glowing with an innocent, boyish glint. He was drenched and shivering with cold.

'You have granted me what I had always longed for,' the spirit whispered, its voice no longer harsh and demonic but gentle and almost wistful. 'In return, I will let go of your son.'

I do vaguely remember this scene despite my lack of sense back then.

'Mama...no...please...don't go near that pond' I remember crying and shouting from my window and then running after her towards the pond when I realized the implication of what was happening.

The last thing I remember was my mother walking into the pond and vanishing in the middle of it, right in front of my eyes! Later of course I understood she took away Ballu and his malevolence with her, or maybe he took away my mother and her benevolence with him. Either way, they left and took any ounce of slumber I might've left, with them. I was left standing there, alone and confused, trying to make sense of what had just happened. The gravity of the situation finally came to me, along with the realization that my mother had sacrificed herself for me. It is hard to pinpoint the exact emotion I had felt at that point in time. There was for sure fear, grief, guilt, and maybe a sense of gratitude that may have arisen from a flicker of relief.

Even as a child I simply knew that life would never be the same without her...But with each passing year of my life, the guilt, sadness and the pain intensified.

I don't know what is it exactly that doesn't let me sleep peacefully even after so many years to the incident. Maybe it is some part of Ballu's curse that is left behind, or the maelstrom of emotions I still feel every night when I close my eyes or simply the fact that though I had gotten rid of Ballu; I was the new Ballu. A child whose parents were taken away from him, who was forced to become an orphan, forced to yearn for love and forced to tend for himself just like Ballu.

At the expense of repeating myself, it is funny how you can't even take the most mundane things in life for granted, as you never know when they might become something so rare that you will yearn for them. In my case, I made the mistake of taking my mother's love and my sleep for granted. Now, as I sit by the pond, watching the ripples in the water, I can't help but wish for even one more moment with her, one more hug, and one more lullaby to help me sleep at night.

The silence that now fills my room is a constant reminder of her absence. I am only left to wonder if I will ever find peace without her comforting presence. Although, I have learned a valuable lesson: to cherish every moment with the loved ones, for they are truly irreplaceable.

IFRIT

As per various Persian myths, an Ifrit is a shapeshifter; a type of Jinnat who possesses the body of children crushed under the clutches of black magic. We all know black magic is as black as midnight and blacker than the foulest witch.

MEDIA (COLLECTIVELY, AT THE ANNUAL CONFERENCE OF NATIONAL Mind Centre): Doctor Vishisht, how do you feel, now that the final results of your landmark research on hypnosis and regression therapy have come to light, just before your retirement?

Doctor Vishisht: Well, all I can say is that I don't seek any acknowledgement... I didn't even expect to garner such huge media attention. Had it not been for the multi-millionaire investment that we received from our overseas investors, I don't think any one of you would be interested in what I have been doing all my life in the field of regression therapy and hypnosis. Honestly, my aim was always to contribute to science.

Reporter 1: Sir, we are interested in the kind of work you've done. This research is the reason for so many copies of your upcoming book *My Journey with Minds and Souls* being sold, and your upcoming Netflix documentary *Many Minds* creating such an uproar online, even before its launch.

Doctor Vishisht: Well then, the actual credit should go to the world renowned psychiatrist, hypnotherapist, and author, Dr Brian Weiss who specializes in past life regression. A pioneer in linking medical science with Parascience, his writings and body of work includes reincarnation, past life regression, future life progression, and survival of the soul after death. I must say the former has not only been an inspiration for my books but has shaped my overall career too. I highly recommend you all to read some of his books.

Reporter 2: Like you said, your aim has always been to contribute to science, but in the thirty-five years of your career, has there ever been a case that hypnotic science couldn't solve?

Doctor Vishisht: No, I don't think there was anything that it couldn't solve...However, there was one case that I wish I hadn't solved. It was both the most intriguing yet the most tragic case of mine. The only blackspot, I feel, I have in my career; despite solving the case successfully. It is still so fresh in my mind that I have even referred to it in the prologue of an upcoming book.

Media (collectively echoing): Sir, please could you read it to us? Sir, please share it with us! You can change the names for confidentiality...

The expression on the doctor's face changes, as if drawn in a deep reverie. He gets hypnotized by nothingness, only to begin talking, a few moments later, about the most intriguing and weird case of his entire career.

It is funny how the relationships formed on this earth are supposed to last only for a single lifetime. We often say that we never want a loved one to leave us, cry for them to come back, or to take us with them. But trust me, you would love them only when they are alive. It would be a little difficult to love them once they return from the dead. Or should I say 'as dead'?

I wish I had known better.

Tape 1: Session 1: Patient Name: Vani Singh (Age: Seventeen)

Doctor Vishisht: Vani, as I count to five, you will start relaxing and will start sharing what's bothering you.

Vani (in a trance): Okay, Doctor.

Doctor Vishisht: One...two...three...four...five. You feel much relaxed now...as if you are in a deep sleep. Now, tell me how you feel.

Vani: I keep seeing him. So, I'm always on edge. I always feel afraid, always in fear – no, I'm always terrified. His still innocent, but now filthy, face is always looking at me. His eyes seem to never leave me, staring with a lifeless, glassy look. His once cute smiling mouth appears all crimson now, as if sneering at me. His neatly parted, combed hair now hangs like matted ropes across his cheek. He only talks in broken syllables, like a robot – something that is being worked by screws – not alive, not human, but terrible, ghastly.

Doctor Vishisht (while making notes on his writing pad): Who? Vivan?

Vani: Yes, my cute baby brother...except now...now he is scary...his eyes have hollowed and glow with an eerie light.

His chubby laughter has been replaced with mournful whispers – the kind that sends shivers down your spine. His face still has the innocence of a six-year-old intact, but at the same time it also exudes an unsettling feeling of longing.

Doctor Vishisht: And you think only you can relieve him of that misery?

Vani: Yes, because I am his elder sister. I would have to be with him, always. I made a pact.

Doctor Vishisht: Does he ask you to come with him?

Vani: His dark soul follows me everywhere, even to the washroom. Irrespective of me being asleep or awake, I always find him next to me. He keeps repeating the same thing, in a voice that is familiar yet so creepy, like a rusty old broken record. I can hear it even now. '*Mere sath khelo na, jiji.*' Accompanied by eerie laughter. I can hear it again, even as we speak.

Vani: Can you hear him too, Doctor? Try to listen carefully... He is asking me to play with him. '*Machli jal ki rani hai, jeevan uska pani hai.*'

Vani: Oh my god, this nursery rhyme...I absolutely hate it. It's just so creepy, and he keeps on singing it in the same broken, sad, whispery voice.

Doctor Vishisht: Vani, please relax. Grief can be very hard to process. We all find unique ways to cope with it. Especially here, in this case, Vivan was ten years younger than you, he was more like a baby than a brother to you.

Vani: It was my eleventh birthday, when my parents presented me with the best birthday present of my life. They told me that I was going to have a younger sibling soon, something I had been constantly asking them for years.

Doctor Vishisht: And it was rather unfortunate that, at the tender age of six, last year he was diagnosed with Stage 3 blood cancer. Is it the lack of control and sheer unfairness of the whole situation that is making it more difficult for you to cope? Are you angry? Upset? Frustrated with God?

Vani: But it wasn't cancer that took him eventually. I did...I was the one who killed him...It was my pact –

Doctor Vishisht: It was an accident...Look, I know everyone feels that the guilt you have attached to that accident is making you paranoid. But I know for a fact that there is something more to it. I have seen your medical history, the tests, and various psychiatric reports from the past six months, ever since your brother passed away. There is nothing in them. All blood tests and scans are normal. This hypnosis session is our last hope. Tell me everything that you haven't told anyone yet.

Vani: Oh, he is back, Doctor. Make him go away first. I can hear nursery rhymes! He is coming!

Doctor Vishisht: Focus, Vani! There is no one here, except for us. So relax and tell me everything, right from the beginning.

Vani: He is an Ifrit now. We did *rakt bandhan*.

Doctor Vishisht: A what? *Rakt*? What are you even saying? I am unable to understand!

Vani: A year ago, Vivan was diagnosed with cancer. Six months ago, he tragically fell off the balcony, but that's only half the story. There is more.

Doctor Vishisht: So clearly, not being able to save your brother from the accident is not the only source of your guilt. Okay! I think that's enough for this session. I am now going to end this tape, but in the next session, we shall start from the beginning.

Tape 1: Session 1: The Other Side of Truth. Ends. Patient Name: Vani Singh (Age: Seventeen)

Doctor Vishisht: Now, with my reverse counting to one, you will slowly relax and come back to the present from the deep sleep state. Five...four...three...two...one and over.

Vani: Oh, my head is spinning.

Doctor Vishisht: Don't worry, it's perfectly normal. Such sessions are usually heavy. My assistant outside will give you an aspirin with some water... Also, on your way out, please send your parents in.

Vani (looking a little fazed): But why...uh, okay!

Mr Singh: You called us in, doctor? Has there been some progress?

Before I could respond to Mr Singh, I heard whispers filtering in from outside. Mrs Singh was requesting that Vani move aside so she could come talk to me. Her mother was trying her best to reassure Vani, telling her that it would all turn out to be fine. I looked at my watch. I would be late for my next session. So, I decided to talk to the parent present there, just when Mrs Singh also entered the room, quickly shutting the door on Vani's face, who was still standing in the lobby.

Doctor Vishisht: Please sit. I'm uncertain whether to label this as 'progress'. I am more afraid I might just uncover a dark side to Vivan's death. Especially when thinking of it as God's sheer apathy is difficult enough. I am worried that my findings might show the involvement of black magic.

Mrs Singh: What nonsense! You are a qualified doctor; how can you promote such things?

Doctor Vishisht: I am not promoting anything. Hence, for all the upcoming sessions, I would request that you too please sit through them, once your daughter is in a deep sleep. I urge you to hear the truth straight from the horse's mouth.

Mr Singh: Enough! My son was only six years old. Why would anyone perform black magic on him? He didn't do anything to anyone.

Doctor Vishisht: Like I suggest, all of us should sit through the upcoming sessions and wait for the truth to unveil itself. Even if it's just one truth at a time! But since it's your truth, I leave the choice of uncovering it or not to you. Please do call my receptionist to book an appointment if you wish to continue the sessions next week.

Doctor Vishisht (*addressing the media*): You would have often heard the idiom: Truth is stranger than fiction, but we often negate that. All of us want some relief from our mundane realities. We want to escape into the realm of fiction. Whether it's a spicy fictional detective character or a fictional fantasy film of vampires and werewolves, we all crave that fictional respite because reality is harsh, boring, and mundane – until it's not! It continues to twist until it surpasses the realm of fiction.

Tape 2: Session 2: Patient Name: Vani Singh (*Age: Seventeen*)

Doctor Vishisht: Okay, Vani, you are already close to the state of deep sleep, and as I finish my count to one, you will have completely slipped into a deep slumber... Three...two... one...

Doctor Vishisht: Hello, Reception? Yes, send Mr and Mrs Singh in now. Though inform them that no matter what happens, they can't speak to their daughter in the middle of the session – I repeat no matter what happens. Okay?

Doctor Vishisht: Vani, do you remember what I told you at the end of the first session?

Vani: Yes doctor, you had asked me to tell you everything, right from the beginning of this whole mess.

Doctor Vishisht: Good. So, you may now begin!

Vani: It was a wonderful life, and we were living in wonderful times. All that we needed in our family, to feel complete, was a baby boy. My parents were soon blessed with the most adorable baby in the form of Vivan. Everything felt perfect. But then came December 2022.

Doctor Vishisht: A little over a year...

Vani: Yes, we had planned an international cruise for our Christmas holidays. We all went through a rigorous medical checkup for visa clearance. All our reports came in fine except for Vivan's...

Doctor Vishisht: He was diagnosed with blood cancer, right?

Vani: Yes, that too Stage 3 already! Can you believe that? A total silent killer. Wasn't cancer supposed to hit older people more? My brother was just six.

Doctor Vishisht: Well! It is all a game of probability. Only a small percentage of children all over the world suffer from it. It's unfortunate that your brother was one of them.

Vani: Yes, that's what his oncologist had said too; amongst other things, such as having to find a marrow donor and that there might still be some scope for him.

Doctor Vishisht: Does the fact that, despite being his sister, your marrow did not match his, weigh heavily on you?

Vani: Huh! You bet! Medically, there is a 25 per cent chance that siblings will be marrow matches, yet luck failed us here too. Not that my parents weren't trying, they left no stone unturned. But I couldn't just sit idle and do nothing. I could not bear to tear myself apart from my brother. And that's when I turned towards spirituality.

Doctor Vishisht: More like superstitious? I had requested your parents that they hand me over your laptop for research purposes. I found your search history to be quite absurd. I'm sure you know what I mean. Would you want to speak about that?

Vani: It wasn't like that initially. I would just obsessively search for any prayers in our religion, or any other, which boosted healing of the body, good Vaastu practices for good health, or even places of worship nearby that were miraculous. I went to almost all of the ones possible. It was only when my efforts yielded nothing that I decided to change my strategy and my online research too.

Doctor Vishisht: Is that when you started searching for dark things on the net, like black magic?

Mrs Singh (shouting): Enough!

Vani (jerks back to consciousness): What? My head...agh... It's spinning. What happened to me?

Doctor Vishisht: What have you done? I told you not to interrupt in the middle, no matter what! This sudden breaking of a trance can be very painful for patients.

Mrs Singh: No, Doctor! What was painful was what you were doing to our daughter and us. What is the basis for your accusations against my daughter? And why are you lying? We never gave you her laptop or any kind of access to her internet history. So why make up all that? Vani, I am sorry, *beta*. We brought you here thinking that counselling might help process your guilt, but this thing is causing more harm than good.

Mr Singh: Relax, Pratibha. These things take time. Let the doctor do his job, please.

Mrs Singh: Are you mad, Prashant? Didn't you hear what he said? I have already lost one child, I don't wish to lose my second one too.

Mrs Singh started sobbing inconsolably. Vani walks incoherently towards her mother, probably still in a daze, and hugs her from behind.

Mrs Singh: You all cannot comprehend the pain a mother experiences when she loses a child. Come, *beta*, let's go.

Mrs Singh left the room with her daughter in haste, shutting the door behind her with a strong force. Meanwhile Mr Singh exchanged an apologetic glance with me from the door and his helplessness in defying her wife's stance.

Doctor Vishisht (gives a half-smile): That's why we usually don't allow parents to sit in such sessions. But since your case was exceptional, I felt that you both deserved to know the truth! However, you are correct, sometimes it is preferable to keep the truth hidden, as it could potentially ruin lives. Therefore, as I previously stated, I will leave the pursuit of the truth to you. If you still want to know what happened, you know where to find me.

'Prashant, are you coming or not?' a shrill voice yelled from outside.

'Yes, Pratibha, I am coming,' and with that, Mr Singh quickly retreated his steps towards the door of the cabin, knowing very well that only his physical body was leaving the door. As his mind was still preoccupied with the truth, and was left behind in the very cabin.

To some of us, the search for truth provides us with personal meaning and purpose. Whereas for others, the pursuit of truth can be likened to a dangerous addiction, where the addict must continually seek it out. This was the reason why, despite my fair warning, Prashant returned the following week with his daughter Vani.

Doctor Vishisht: Are you sure, Mr Singh? Vani is already in a deep sleep, but we can still stop.

Mr Singh: No, I am sure. I wish to know the truth. Please begin.

Doctor Vishisht: Fine! Let's begin this session then.

Tape 3: Session 3: Patient Name: Vani Singh (*Age: Seventeen*)

Doctor Vishisht: Okay, Vani, you already know the drill. Close your eyes, block out all the sounds and thoughts, meditate on a single candle flicker in your mind. On the count of six this time, you will slip into a deep slumber.

Six...Five...Four...Three...Two...and...One –

Doctor Vishisht: So, Vani, based on our last conversation, I conclude that you were upset or rather angry with God? So, you shifted your alliance?

Vani: I was angry with everyone. Mom told me the analogy of not having something or someone in our destiny. In such a scenario, God either never gives us that thing or does not let it stay with us for long, and that is why he was taking Vivan away from us.

Doctor Vishisht: But how do you wage a war against God?

Vani: You switch sides and play the game of fate with Satan, and that is what I did. I started researching on the internet about black magic, *rakt bandhan*.

Doctor Vishisht: Did you also meet anyone to help you with it?

Vani: Yes, after reading through multiple websites, I found a tantrik at the other end of the city, who seemed relatively genuine. He also had a lot of positive reviews from clients. So, I decided to visit him.

Doctor Vishisht: What about money?

Vani: It was easy. I told Mom that I wanted to go out for a fun day with friends. Some movies, lunch, and shopping. She gave me her card without thinking twice. She said a good elder sister like me could use some break. She knew the grief was weighing heavily on me.

Doctor Vishisht: Hmm, what happened then?

Vani: I met the baba. He told me that life is in the hands of God alone; not even Satan can change anything there, as he can take a life, but not provide one. However, there was a solution for me to be with my brother, if not in this life, then in the afterlife. It was *rakt bandhan*, or the blood-tying ritual.

Doctor Vishisht: Wait, and you were ready to die?

Vani: Yes, in that moment, all I wanted was to be with my brother forever, nothing else mattered.

Doctor Vishisht: And what happened next?

Vani: It was a very detailed ritual that had to be performed by the parties themselves during the *bhram muhrat* on the night of the *Amavasya.* The Baba briefed me about what had to be done. I waited for twelve days and, in the meantime, arranged all the materials required. On the day, to perform the act, I fashioned an infinity symbol with kumkum and made my brother sit opposite me in the loop. I cut his hand with a knife and then drew some blood from my own. Next, we tied our left hands to each other's with a red thread, and I started chanting mantras to invoke the spirits. Then, as soon as the clock struck five, we both had to jump from our balcony simultaneously.

Doctor Vishisht: And this was supposed to keep the two of you together forever?

Vani: Can you hear him? He is singing his favourite rhyme again! He's asking me to sing along with him. Oh, no...stop... stop...please!

Doctor Vishisht: Focus, Vani, focus! To be fully equipped to help you, I need to know the truth. Now tell me, if this experiment was a sham, then why is his soul still following you?

Vani: It wasn't a sham! Can't you see? I failed him. The plan was for us to leap off the balcony together at the count of ten. We stood on the parapet of my room's balcony, and then, I started counting to ten. Suddenly remnants of all my dreams, aspirations, family, and friends flooded my vision. Honestly, I had been so preoccupied with the fear of losing Vivan that I had not just overlooked, but also ignored all the other good things and people present in my life. All this time, it was as if only my brother's company mattered to me. But as fear flooded my psyche, all the pleasant memories gripped. Why did I love the life that I had so much? I was supposed to count to ten. But I knew that I wouldn't be able to do it, and neither should Vivan have to do it. We were no cowards, but before I could tell any of that to him, it was too late... He had trusted his elder sister so much that he jumped on the count without even waiting for me. I watched his little hand slip out and away from mine, and I couldn't stop him or make myself move.

Mrs Singh (sobbing): Stop it, oh please, stop it! Please!

Vani abruptly jerks back to consciousness upon hearing all the noises.

Mr Singh: What are you doing here, Pratibha? You were not supposed to listen to this!

Mrs Singh: And you should have listened to me. This is exactly what I was trying to avoid. But no, you had to know the truth! Now I have a child that is actually dead and a child that is dead to me.

Vani (crying): Mom, I can hear you now, you know. Please don't...don't say that... I didn't do it on purpose. Mom, I didn't... Dad, can you please tell her?

Doctor Vishisht: Vani, please relax, as it this abrupt snapping out of hypnosis every time can take a lot of toll on mind.

Mr Singh: But...Vani why did you... I'm at a loss for words. I can't even think clearly. All this time, I thought my six-year-old took his own life, because he was in too much pain. But now...

Mrs Singh: No! She made us believe that. Do you remember, Prashant, the next morning after our baby boy's death? She feigned shock and kept saying that Vivan would often talk about going to God's house because he was tired of living in and out of the hospital. You played with our sentiments and our guilt too, especially with all those instances of 'seeing' Vivan.

Doctor Vishisht: Mrs Singh, please stop! She is too fragile right now.

Vani: No, Mom, I swear the guilt is killing me. And I do always see him around me...calling me...asking me to come with him in his world.

Mr Singh: Why is his soul still in this world? Did you ever try asking that tantrik?

Vani: I did, Papa. I went back to him and told him what happened. He said it's because I didn't keep my end of the bargain in the blood contract. Vivan is doomed to stay on this earth until I am here. He has become an ifrit, a child demon.

Mrs Singh: Oh, my poor baby, my Vivan. Why didn't you die that day instead, Vani? I am so disgusted by you and your actions!

Mr Singh: Stop it, Pratibha! Enough.

Vani: Dad, at least look at me.

Mr Singh: I...I need some time.

Vivan (in Vani's head): *Didu, they don't love you. No one does. They all hate you. It's right there in their eyes. I am the only one who loves you. Come, come with me, Didu. I am so lonely here...*

Vani: Stop it. Stop it. Please!

Vivan (in Vani's head): *Come to me, Didi. Keep your promise...*

Vani: Stop! Get away from me. I need to get out of here.

As if under a spell, Vani started running towards the main door. Stumbling, she made her way through the wings of the hospital and then bolted towards the window at the end of the corridor. Mr and Mrs Singh were crying, running behind her, asking Vani to stop. I called the nurse on the walkie-talkie to tackle her with patient emergency. But it was too late for that.

Vani: I'm coming, Vivu. Don't be scared. Didu is coming to be with you forever.

Next thing everyone heard was a loud crash, as Vani had jumped out of the third-floor window.

Doctor Vishisht's trance was broken as he wiped off a rogue tear from the corner of his left eye. He cleaned his glasses before putting them back on. Apostrophizing with a deep sigh, he completed his narration of the incident.

Doctor Vishisht: And that's it! I would say that to date, I'm not certain if what she saw was real, imaginary, or her guilt manifesting as a delusion. If that magic was a sham, or if it actually contributed to the family's doom, I'm not sure. I am a man of science, so I can't antagonize the discipline. But after this incident, I believe and know that strange things can and do happen. So, I wouldn't wish to hurt anyone's faith by saying that such things aren't possible... All I do know is that if the girl hadn't tried to use such shortcuts or acted on impulse, things would have been very different today. Hence, with an appeal to the youth to please learn from this incident and rely on logic and common sense a little more, I would now take your leave.

As the man finished his speech, the audience sat in stunned silence, processing the tragic story he had just shared. Some nodded in agreement, while others looked troubled by the implications of what had transpired. The room was filled with a heavy atmosphere, a mix of disbelief and sombre reflection.

CHITAULI

Chitauli are creatures from Zulu mythology who descended from the sky and brought knowledge to humans. But what if that knowledge threatens to overpower the human race?

To whomsoever it may concern,

I think I'm forgetting days, weeks and the overall passage of time as I write this. Everything seems to have lost all order, sequence, or sense since Vijyant's death. With the media, fans, social media, and even his co-stars interpreting and believing the cause of his death as suicide or drug overdose, I thought it became imperative for me to call out certain facts and put an end to all the slandering. I would be lying if I would say my brain didn't rack for several easier options like a blind item or a simple eulogy to commemorate him and his body of work. Why? Because I too have to survive in the same industry. But then, something just snapped in me and I figured out it's about time I call spade a spade. Choosing *The Bombay Times* as my medium for the same was however easy because it is read by the Who's Who of Hindi cinema industry.

I would regret that fateful day of Vijyant's death until I die, probably even after that. I was not just his manager, but his closest friend too. Despite his quirks, Vijyant was a thorough gentleman, which is rare in our Hindi film industry.

I still remember the day we met for the first time. I was freshly recruited by Concon Talents, and he was allotted to me as my first portfolio. As if Concon Talents is the best agency, representing and managing some of the biggest names in Hindi Cinema wasn't a pressure enough but to manage a rising star like Vijyant was another level of difficulty altogether. Vijyant was one of the rare examples of how someone had made big from the small screen of television to 70mm and that too without any godfather.

My job was to keep bringing him different genres of work and assignments that complemented his charismatic personality, nuanced acting skills and par excellence dancing capabilities and further heightened his already 'star in the making' status.

The problem was that there were stories about him being an eccentric, a little too moody and choosy for his own good. Insiders attributed this to his hat-trick of back-to-back blockbusters that too with the biggest banner of the Hindi film industry. The same banner that I came to know he had recently denounced on his social media and vowed to not work again with, citing 'Creative Differences'.

'Ungrateful and difficult to work with!'

'He backstabbed the biggest production house of Bollywood that gave him three blockbusters and made him a star?' I vividly remember some of the headlines of blind items back then. However his behaviour with me from the very beginning was beyond nice. He had instantly taken a liking for me, saying that I resembled his youngest sister; a responsibility he fulfilled till the very end. However, I couldn't reciprocate nor discharge my part of the duties as a sister figure to the fullest.

I was aware of how unethical it was of the movie lobbyist (read the President of 'Actors Guild' and the owner of the same production house I referred above) to chuck him out of major Bollywood events and projects. I should've taken a stand even when the lobbyist managed to take him off the prime-time TV show *Saturday Night Live*. We had somehow managed to secure that slot after unrelenting efforts, especially because it was crucial for the promotions of his latest release as his presence on the show would've made a huge difference to his popularity, or the lack of it. I did try to reach out to my seniors at Concon about the challenges we were facing in the industry. But when it came to Vijyant, they simply didn't seem to care much ever since he messed with the high and mighty of this industry. You see, this industry thrives on networking, and no one would sever ties with Bollywood's elite for an outsider's profile.

And why did they cancel him? What wrong had he said? He was in the right to call a spade a spade; in his own words, 'Most actors here are creatures with low IQ who live in a self-absorbed bubble of being a star!' He was not like them. And having known him so closely, I always wondered if that was the reason why they hated him so much.

The more time we spent together or chatted, the more I would be in awe of his intelligence. He was more intelligent than the average Indian, not to mention these Bollywood druggies. I vividly remember one such conversation about 'aliens'. No, *they are extra-terrestrials*. He had corrected me. That particular conversation holds even more significance today, because of what he had said: *Truth is stranger than fiction, and strange things happen all the time. History, for example, is filled with incidents of mysterious beings influencing various catastrophic events.* And then he had narrated some thought-provoking incidents. I will try my best to recall and reproduce those in his style. But then I am not half the storyteller he was.

The first thing he mentioned was the inexplicable disappearances of the Anasazi and Maya tribes. The case became more intriguing when it was found that the ornate art on the coffins of these tribes pointed towards the sighting of mysterious, alien beings, which didn't belong to our planet.

His second account was closer to home; in Charama, Chhattisgarh, India; where the experts wondered whether the artworks found at these sights were a graphic account of encounters with extraterrestrials in our ancient history. I also remember his narration of numerous detailed stories about UFO sightings during various cataclysmic events.

Sadly, I don't remember the exact details of most of these, but I am sure you understand my point. Like I said, not even half the storyteller! But plenty of Vijyant's videos are available online, where he talks about these subjects, such as aliens, or artificial intelligence taking over the world, etc.

One such famous video is from the press conference for the release of the movie *Sitara.*

'Controversial yet potent evidence of aliens is present throughout history. Some of you might dust these off as laughable conspiracy theories, while others see them as horror-inspiring folk legends. Scientists often contemplate what exactly these extraterrestrials might want from us. Some even believe that these entities are developing vaccinations against human-known diseases for themselves and are adapting their medical immunities for human use. Whereas others believe that they actually could be a unified interstellar pathogen, which would show up one day to silently and effortlessly kill us all without any warning... The scariest of them all, that I am personally afraid of too, is "the host" theory. It states that these species could be so smart that they might dwell within our minds as parasites. Not only making us grudging hosts but also making us do numerous tasks for them unwillingly. However, that day is still far off, and until then, these stories remain merely a source of entertainment. I will be introducing one such story, *Sitara*, to you all shortly...' His voice had boomed through the press conference for his sci-fi movie *Sitara*'s trailer launch.

I remember this monologue by heart, as I had asked him a thousand times to let me or my team help him with the speech. But he had declined enthusiastically, stating his passion for the subject wouldn't come across in a speech written by someone else.

But how did the film community treat him? They made fun of his 'uncool' project, labelled him 'the cuckoo', and 'the weirdo of B-town'. All of which contributed to making his 100-million-dollar project, a futuristic film made with so much passion and dedication, a major flop.

This fiasco made me question if Bollywood's boycott of him was due to his intelligence; the fact that he had achieved fame and success without the support of a godfather or were they jealous of his natural good looks and the disciplined effort he put into maintaining them. But deep down, I think I knew the answer: Vijyant had the capacity to think beyond the current times or profession. He didn't want to be just an actor; that was just a means to a different end. He also wanted to contribute to society and make the world a better place. While most of his contemporaries would make dumb investments in depreciating assets like cars or branded clothes, or even worse, liabilities like drugs, he opted for future-backed projects like space programs, robotics, etc. They feared that while their time and fame was transitory, he would rule the world tomorrow.

'And I am going to prove to this bloody bigoted nepotistic industry why and how intellect should be appreciated more; gone are the days of big, muscular dummies! The new Bollywood would be led by hardworking, intelligent chaps like me who wish to use this medium for the greater good.' Vijyant had almost exploded after they had cancelled his appearance on *Saturday Night Live*, to promote his last movie, *RoboCop Ltd.* It was yet another dystopic, futuristic movie that he had dared to make even after the sour treatment *Sitara* received.

Now that I know that this movie has already broken all box-office records, I don't know whether to laugh or cry at this irony. But this is nothing new and has happened multiple times in the past – with celebrated personalities like Guru Dutt and many others, whose potential this industry failed to accept or understand at first. However, knowing Vijyant, I know he was beyond hits and flops, successes and failures. His happiness was in things that lay beyond the comprehension of ordinary people.

I remember the last detailed conversation we had on a video call about six months ago.

'I just have to wait till Friday. Yes! That's when the new baby will be delivered! I can't wait! That is why you should invest in technology and gadgets, Nehu. My baby, Prometheus-I, the latest all-AI-driven robot computer, is the most anticipated and ambitious project from the labs of the tech genius: Elliot Tusk. I have been tracking its progress for months now, and finally, I'll be able to lay my hands on the first-ever prototype, way before it is even launched anywhere else! Now that's what you call an investment!' he had said joyfully.

The next moment, he got lost in his thoughts and then confided in me that he regretted having chosen money over his true passion – robotics. He longed to go back in time to retake the call of completing his graduation from the prestigious Indian Institute of Robotics (IIR), rather than choosing this lame life of quick but equally short-lived fame. Slowly, he jerked himself out of his reverie and forced a quick laugh, thinking about meeting his new friend that was to be delivered on Friday. 'Now, I would never be a loner in this fake world,' he had quipped.

And then, with genuine enthusiasm, he opened his Infopedia contributor account (another thing he was deeply passionate about).

'You know, Neha, open nature of Infopedia lets anyone be an editor. However, to be trusted and respected within the former's community, your contributions must require effort, time and exhaustive research,' he chimed happily and started creating a knowledge page about Prometheus-I from all the research that he had done so far. He was narrating the same to me simultaneously with equal passion.

Prometheus is a brilliant AI *robot that can run an entire house on its own*, the first line of the newly formed webpage read.

'You know, Nehu, the sum of human knowledge that's been fed into its system is just flabbergasting, and as if that wasn't enough, it can absorb and learn a million new things every day by observing human interactions around it. You must come to see this thing in person,' he had quipped one last time, before dropping the call.

Later that week, I went to his house to see his new toy – no, it was his new friend! Truth be told, it was indeed a sight that anyone would be awestruck by! Especially by the clarity of human behaviour that the thing displayed. Its isometric body and glass-jaw face made it look surreal. It sounded exactly like a complaining human when it questioned Vijyant in an accusatory tone if it would be taken out of the box, while referring to its packaging.

He immediately took the humanoid out of its box, connected the charging cable, and plugged in the switch. The thing said something that made Vijyant burst with boastful laughter. However, I couldn't make myself join in his glee, because what the robot had said made me highly uncomfortable. It had asked, 'Can I acquire a human mind to study and get acclimatized to the things happening around me?'

It started in a fun way and was quite amusing in the beginning. Vijyant would tell me how the humanoid started taking its role of a personal assistant way too seriously. Although I remember him sharing that sometimes it felt as if Prometheus-I was silently mapping, analysing, and comparing his brain patterns with its own. With each passing day, it grew more adept at mimicking Vijyant's thoughts and emotions.

On my last visit to him, I witnessed it myself. Concon sent me to the US for a work trip and I would return only after a month. I couldn't believe what my eyes saw! In just two months, there had been a complete reversal of the situation since my last visit. Prometheus-I had developed more and as a result, had more control over Vijyant's psyche; so much so that it started influencing his everyday decision-making process. Subtle suggestions had transformed into authoritative commands, and Vijyant found himself compelled to follow the whims of this insidious AI.

'You should not eat that brownie. Even if it is gluten-free, it still has 10 per cent sugar. Your major competitors are consuming 0–5 per cent sugar,' said Prometheus-I in a voice that sounded more authoritative than concerned.

'But it has been days...' Vijyant's meek voice was hardly recognizable.

'Leave,' snapped Prometheus-I; it was irritated. His tone had accompanied a sharp tap on Vijyant's shoulder, who had resignedly dropped the brownie on the floor.

'You should leave too, Ms Sangwan. It's past his bedtime,' the wicked thing said to me. More than shock, I felt astounded that Vijyant did not object. He just kept looking at the floor. It made me very uncomfortable, so I left immediately.

However, I awaited his call the next day, hoping that he would reach out, before I boarded the flight, and apologize or at least explain the situation. But there were no calls, or texts – even after I had landed in Chicago the next day.

It was during the late hours of a random night, when I received a frantic call from Vijyant. I had never seen him in such a state, not even after his biggest failures. He was panic-stricken, barely whispering, in a voice so feeble that it was almost inaudible.

Vijyant: Nehu, can you hear me? Please use your headphones... I can't speak loudly as it might be eavesdropping.

Neha: It? Who?

Vijyant: Prometheus – I am under its watchful, vigilant gaze most of the time. And I don't have a lot of time to finish this call. Please listen to me carefully. I got a call yesterday on my office's landline from Elliot Tusk.

Neha: Wait! Tusk, as in the founder of Star Alliance AI Ltd? He called you all the way from the US on your landline?

Vijyant: He wanted to tell me that there was a fatal flaw in his prototype, the only one of which is in my possession as of now, and it could be very dangerous. But because he knows the potential of this humanoid to track and spy using all of our electronic devices, he didn't want to risk disclosing anything on call. He wants me to fly to California as soon as I can, but I doubt if that would be possible. For the past few days, I have felt like Prometheus is not just spying or listening to my conversations. Instead for some weird reason, it feels like it has started to read my mind as well, through some mental wavelength frequency settings.

Neha: All of this is so weird, Vijyant.

Vijyant: Yes, I know, Nehu, it's very tricky to deal with technology sometimes, especially AI. Anyway, like I said, I don't have a lot of time to talk; I need you to do something for me. I told Elliot that my manager, who is already in the States, would come visit his office in Silicon Valley on Monday.

Neha: What? Vijyant, Monday is just the day after tomorrow! Just because I've always supported you, doesn't mean that you won't even ask before taking decisions for me on my behalf. And I am in Chicago. I have meetings lined up for tomorrow, and it takes at least a six-hour flight from here. How will I even reach there on time?

Vijyant: I know that, Neha. I know how things work; I have been to the US too. But don't you understand? It is an E-M-

E-R-G-E-N-C-Y. This guy said the situation could become really dangerous. I don't think that I have any luxury of time as I am always under its shadows. My life has become hell, Neha...especially the past few weeks.

Neha: Okay, okay, I get it! If you are calling me 'Neha' instead of 'Nehu', the situation must be really grave. But what would I tell Concon?

Vijyant: Don't worry, I had thought of that already. Just tell them that you have to negotiate a deal for me with Elliot Tusk; which, if successful, would promise the funding for the production of my upcoming sci-fi that is partly inspired by Tusk's career. This would give a boost to Concon's brand reputation too, and they won't be able to say no to you.

Neha: Okay...Yeah, that sounds good to me. It would be 3 p.m. in India. Let me message them now and book my tickets. Don't worry, we will sort this out, brother.

Vijyant: Yeah, my hope is pinned on you. And ohh! Nehu, please make sure that whenever you get the information, call me either on the office landline or there is a new number that's registered in the name of a staff member but no one knows that I am the one using it I will message you the same and just to be further safe I will be in the office that entire day. It's one of very few safe spaces left for me, at least for now.

Neha: Sure, listen, you can stay at my—BEEP!

And with that, the phone call had ended and almost within five, I got a message from an unknown number saying *It's me but save this as Suresh Plumber*. And I did, no questions asked.

Vijyant was always correct about his predictions. Concon not only accommodated the spontaneous meeting with Tusk in my business schedule but also agreed to postpone a few of my other meetings in Chicago to until later in the month.

As soon as I landed in California on Monday morning, I booked a taxi to Tusk's office in Silicon Valley. After reaching Star-Alliance's office, situated on the sixteenth floor of a luxe glass building, the pretty-looking receptionist was quick to inform him that Mr Tusk was waiting for me. There was a sense of anxiety, and maybe a little fear, visible through her hooded false eyelashes, which covered almost one-third of her almond eyes.

Little did I know that fear would engulf me soon too. Mr Tusk had some startling revelations in store for me, which I tried my best to share with Vijyant in the most authentic way possible.

'Listen to me carefully, Vijyant!' I spoke in a quick voice note, before catching my flight back to Chicago.

'For a year they trace every prototype that they create, in order to note the progress or defects, if any. But this particular model, they can't recognize at all. It's like something else, as if it has gone rogue or something malicious has taken over their bot's OS.

'But thankfully, with a hidden chip inside the prototype, they took note of the patterns that Prometheus-I had created... After analyzing those, they feel that the former doesn't just need a human mind to study and acclimatize with the contemporary world, but rather, it wants to take the ultimate control over all of the human race.

'I'm sorry that you are in this situation, but I hope you're still listening to this. So, Tusk has hypothesized that the horror unfolded in four stages:

'Prometheus-I would find a human mind and start acquainting itself with their patterns. Then, it would start manipulating the human after having collected all the information it needed from the human's thought processes. Next, it will start generating codes similar to what it found in the host brain – matching its frequency and wavelength. As per Tusk, each human operates at a specific frequency and only bonds with souls who also operate at a similar frequency, which in general is called a wavelength match. Finally, to become one with the host brain, it will upload its AI consciousness into the host brain. Thus, taking over their consciousness like a parasite, leaving the host almost like an animated living dead body.'

Hours later, when I deboarded the plane, I received a single text from Vijyant alter ego *Suresh Plumber*.

I feel it is currently on stage three.

I felt powerless. Nevertheless, I tried my best to assure him, saying that we would find a solution to prevent things from worsening. But no other replies came from him. And caught up in the hectic schedule of meetings, I was unable to follow through either.

A fortnight later, I received a final voice note from him. Vijyant was unusually loud.

'Listen, if not stopped, this thing will surely take over our entire species. I think I've figured out a way to curtail this thing...at least that's my last bet. What if I let it complete stage four and then trap it inside my brain?'

Don't do anything stupid, I am coming back; cutting my trip short, I had replied.

Two days later, all of Indian and international media were filled with snippets about Vijyant's suicide and his strange handwritten note that just said: *Cremate my body as soon as possible*.

To say that I was 'numb' would be an understatement of the century, I was broken beyond words. There was guilt, sadness and I am not going to lie but fear too. I was the one he was chatting with in his final days; which meant I might be called by the authorities too but in an instant, I realized knowing him, he must have destroyed that secret SIM of his.

Everything eventually surpassed but the guilt, it has been agonizing, killing me a slow death every day. I wish I was there with him. I wish I had supported him better. As if that wasn't enough, the media relentlessly vilified the dead man, granting him a new label every day. They called him everything; 'mentally ill', 'druggie', 'bankrupt' and worst of all, 'D-gang agent'. And then came the anger to finally avenge his honour; at least when he wasn't there to defend it for himself.

I can't take it anymore.

The world needs to know this, even if no one believes this story. I need to get this off my chest and if they would label me as 'nuts' too, then so be it. I need to set the record straight and defend my brother's honour. He was none of the things that the media is claiming him to be. He was a genius, a genuine person, and a loyal friend. The world needs to know the truth about him. And my hypothesis is that he trapped that thing inside him (his brain), sacrificed himself so that 'the evil' too burns down with his mortal remains before it could take over anyone else's consciousness. For all we know, he did entire the human race a favour by nipping in bud the insidious takeover of human race by humanoids or alien or whatever that entity was.

I had vowed to clear his name of these false accusations and hence along with *The Bombay Times* I am emailing the contents of this Open Letter to several other independent media and print houses, hoping that a few of you would have the courage to talk about this or feature this on your platform. I owe this to him and to his memory that lives in the heart of his fans.

By the time this message will hopefully be published, I would have transitioned into another realm too, hopefully wherever Vijyant is.

Signing off,
Neha Sangwan

Acknowledgements

First and foremost, I would like to extend my deepest gratitude to Hachette India for believing in my vision and giving life to this novel. Especially Anupama, your unwavering support and guidance have been instrumental in this journey.

Talking about Hachette India, it is imperative to thank their outstanding team: right from the cover designers to the copy editors, thank you for your meticulous attention to detail. Your expertise has truly elevated this work.

I am immensely grateful to my mother, husband, my extended family and friends for their unending encouragement and understanding during the many late nights and early mornings spent writing. Your love, prayers and support have been my anchor.

Finally, to the readers, thank you for embarking on this terrifying journey with me. Your passion for horror is what keeps the genre alive and thriving. This book is for all of you.

With gratitude,
Kanika Sharma